Cloaked by the darkness, soothed by it, she removed her coverall and again fastened herself down. She stretched sensuously. So this was sensory deprivation.

With no sense of time passing she gazed contentedly, languorously at the jewel-laden world swirling beyond the windows, its treasures drifting unawares into the ship's storage containers. She wondered if she could have dreamed her memories, those impossible sensations of the night before.

Drake spoke her name from across the room. "How very lovely you look," she added, amusement in her soft tones.

How can she possibly see me from where she is, Harper wondered, straining to make out any image of her. And then the thought passed from her as Drake reached her, bent down to unfasten the restraint. Harper floated up and into her arms.

Drake murmured, "We have only a few more hours . . . Then I must take care of my ship. . ."

KATHERINE V. FORREST

DREAMS AND SWORDS

The Naiad Press, Inc.
1987

Printed in the United States of America
First Edition

Cover design by Women's Graphic Center
Typesetting by Sandi Stancil

"Xessex" first appeared in *The Magazine of Fantasy & Science Fiction* February 1983
(Copyright © 1983 by Mercury Press, Inc.)

Library of Congress Cataloging in Publication Data

Forrest, Katherine V., 1939—
    Dreams and swords / by Katherine V. Forrest.
        p.   cm.
    Contents: The gift — Jessie — Benny's place —
Xessex — Force majeur — Mother was an alien —
Mandy Larkin — Survivor — O captain, my
captain — The test.
    ISBN 0-941483-03-7
    1. Science fiction, American.   2. Detective and mystery
stories, American.   I. Title.
PS3556.O737D7   1987
813'.54—dc19   87-22447
                                                                            CIP

ACKNOWLEDGEMENTS

With love and appreciation to the Third Street Writers Group — Montserrat Fontes, Janet Gregory Kunert, Jeffrey N. McMahan, Karen Sandler, Naomi Sloan, Gerald Citrin — whose caring and honesty have helped with this collection and all my work.

Special added thanks to Jeff McMahan — his own fine work provided both inspiration and source material for "O Captain, My Captain."

My thanks also to Harriet Clare, whose love for the poetry of Amy Lowell inspired the name "Dreams and Swords" for her bookstore in Indianapolis, IN, and the title for this collection.

BOOKS BY KATHERINE V. FORREST

CURIOUS WINE
DAUGHTERS OF A CORAL DAWN
AMATEUR CITY
AN EMERGENCE OF GREEN
MURDER AT THE NIGHTWOOD BAR
DREAMS AND SWORDS

To Sheila . . .
My dream, my reality

CONTENTS

All books are either dreams or swords....

—Amy Lowell
Sword Blades and Poppy Seed

THE GIFT

The Tehachapi mountains had been selected for the rendezvous. Behind Marge Bowman and Karla Cooper lay the high-rise glitter of Los Angeles; ahead, the humble lights of Bakersfield. The night was cool, crystalline, the stars abundant and close, the summer smell of cooling earth rich and vivid.

The two women had been in their designated place since six o'clock, only two hours early for the rendezvous; but they had come from Oregon — not nearly so far as the other parents — to this single site in the United States, one of ten around the globe. Thousands of parents were gathered along the foothills, but only intermittent murmurs of voices nearby reached Marge and Karla.

Marge pointed a trembling finger at the TV display. "Julie looks so frightened."

Karla did not glance at the screen; through binoculars she stared at the floodlit plain below. She shifted the glasses from the spaceship, pulsing its midnight blue rhythms several miles away, over the thousands of tiny figures populating the plain, to their daughter's compound. "The Monitors are doing their best. Soon it'll be over. Soon, Margie."

Marge said more calmly, "It's going to be worse when the Monitors leave, when it . . . happens."

"Margie, I know," she said helplessly. "I know."

On the screen before Marge Bowman, in slow pan over the children in compound 20D, the remote-controlled camera picked up the face of their daughter — pale, frightened, her blonde silk hair blowing in the cool breeze flowing over the plain. Julie was wearing a warm jacket and pants, but she had apparently lost or discarded her cap. She scanned the plain anxiously, staring at the mountains toward Marge, then twisted to gaze at the distant blinking ship. The Monitor, a young woman in a belted white suit with a red band on the sleeve, came to Julie, knelt and encircled her with an arm.

Marge gazed at her sturdy, beautiful daughter. Julie had been born prematurely — but physically perfect — and had always been small, and beautiful. Unusually beautiful, all the doctors had agreed. Julie hugged the Monitor, her smile radiant; as the camera panned past her, she looked into the lens with wide, vacant blue eyes.

Only one month ago they had met with the Western Director of *Project Transfer*. "Four to seven are the optimum ages, the highest probability — they've established that conclusively," Doctor Morton had told them. "Any younger, the child is too unformed to withstand the shock, the pain. Any older, the biological changes will have destroyed the compatibility. Consequently, Julie will never have another chance."

"The pain," Marge Bowman had said.

"The pain will be extreme. To the farthest limit of tolerance. The process involves imprinting upon the neurological system, and the Mirilians have told us the children cannot be tranquilized. There is no other way. There is nothing to be done about the pain. Talk to the psychologists, the scientists working on the project. Marge, Karla, you have one month to decide whether you want your child to be part of *Project Transfer*. One month."

Karla watched her daughter; watched her pull the hair of a boy of perhaps five with red curls, who whirled to Julie. Julie hugged him, laughing.

Karla whispered, "I love her so. Oh God, how I love her."

Staring at the screen, Marge murmured, "I don't know . . . I just don't know . . . "

"Margie, we've discussed it. Decided." But Karla's voice was tired; and she was uncertain, even now.

"Look." Marge pointed at the screen.

In compound 20D, a Monitor, a dark-haired young woman, was gently and carefully tucking a small, crying boy into a gaily colored conveyance that looked like a toy helicopter. The Monitor straightened, raised both arms; the remote controlled toy-like copter rose, soared toward Marge and Karla and the mountains. "See?" Marge said. "Another recall, there've been *dozens*, Karla. Lots of other parents are changing their minds. We can too. There's still time, right up to . . . the moment."

"Is there anything we haven't gone over?" Karla's fingers traced, circled the recall button on the TV console. "If there's a conceivable reason to change our minds, let's give the signal — have the Monitors return Julie to us."

But there was no reason they hadn't discussed. Endlessly. Exhaustively. They had argued with all the psychologists, the scientists. Talked with each other late into the nights. Awakened at predawn hours to talk still more. Karla could not now remember which objections each had raised, who of them had answered:

"She's our only child, both of us are too old to conceive another."

"For that very reason we owe her whatever we can give — the best springboard possible for her life."

"It's dangerous. It's never been done before."

"The Mirilians are advanced far beyond us. Look at their technology, what they've already given us as a gesture of good will. They tell us it's eighty percent probability — and they're risking their own children, too."

"They also tell us there's a ten percent chance of insanity. A ten percent chance Julie may die."

"But an eighty percent chance for success. A *good* chance. Her *only* chance."

"God gave her to us the way she is, with her limitations."

"The children of Mirilius, are they not also God's creatures?"

"But we love her the way she is . . . Maybe we love her more . . . "

"Are we thinking of Julie, or ourselves?"

On the screen Julie was again looking toward the mountains — toward Marge and Karla — with frightened, bewildered eyes.

The loving sweetness of my daughter, Karla thought. The way she can almost tear the heart out of my chest . . . She'll be forever changed . . . "Why is it taking so long," she demanded in a surge of anger. "Their ship's been here more than an hour. How long do they think we can keep thousands of children calm?"

"Karla, they're doing what we had to do. Saying goodbye to their own children."

But at first, Marge reflected, it had been hard to ascribe feelings to the Mirilians. What they looked like — *that* had taken some getting used to.

The scientists, candid about all aspects of the project, had shown both women holographs of a huge lethal planet of methane and fluoride, and its inhabitants: awesome creatures, easily dominant on their world, stork-like, with one huge green eye, a cruel predatory beak, an immense torso, two powerful limbs that propelled them at breakneck speed over their forbidding terrain.

Dr. Francona had said, "The one essential they have in common with us is love for their young — even more so than we. Mistreatment of offspring is inconceivable. Love for their young is their single greatest outpouring of racial psychic energy, the highest value in their culture."

The psychologist had said, "The Mirilians are completely dissimilar biologically, but they discovered during visits over the last three centuries that the neural structure and circuitry of our bodies and theirs is virtually identical in the first stages of life.

"The greatest tragedy on their world is an infant born physically damaged. It is doomed. On Mirilius, there are no *degrees* of health as we know it. The body of a damaged infant withers and dies, dissolved by their pitiless atmosphere. But only the body dies. The infant metamorphoses into this."

Dr. Francona displayed another holograph to Marge and Karla, cross-shaped spokes of light, ice blue and glowing with energy. "To us this looks like electricity. But it's life, and intelligence. But life doesn't last very long — less than one of our Earth years. With the dawning and growth of intelligence, the infant becomes fully aware of its loss, and grieves and longs for a physical body. The infant eventually relinquishes its will to live."

The scientist had said, "The Mirilians have visited us several times earlier in our history — in the ninth and sixteenth centuries as well as the last three. They're appalled by our history and culture, and would never have made themselves known to us except for their discovery about our children. But they'll return every year if this project is successful, to share more of their knowledge and to continue the project. They have decided to take a chance on us by trusting us with their greatest value — their children."

The screen Marge was watching flashed red. A soft voice announced: "The signal has come from the Mirilian ship. Two minutes."

Through the binoculars, Karla watched the fine blonde hair blow across the forehead of her daughter. She lowered the glasses and swallowed. Tears blurred her vision.

Marge watched the screen; the Monitor knelt beside Julie, hugged her sturdy shoulders, smiled goodbye. Then the Monitor stood, touched a stud on the belt of her white suit. Julie and the other children stared open-mouthed as she floated upward, joined hundreds of other Monitors who drifted gracefully over the plain to the slopes of the mountains, wingless white birds propelled by gravibelt, a gift from the Mirilians.

An opening appeared in the side of the Mirilian ship, a dazzling brilliance in the dark night.

"Karla," Marge whispered.

She flung her arms around Marge; they stood watching, not the screen, but the vast floodlit plain below crowded with Earth children.

Spokes of electric blue light poured from the ship, became wheels of blue flame whirling over the flat plain at incredible speeds under the star-flung sky. From the plain, from the thousands of milling children, rose faint cries.

Karla's eyes were drawn irresistibly to the screen. Amid the terrorized children in compound 20D, Julie stood rooted, hypnotized by horror, mouth open in a scream, not heeding the glancing blow from the boy with red hair who ran into her as he fled the onrushing spokes of blue light.

"Julie," Karla said. She suddenly shouted, "No! Not Julie!"

From all around them came moans and cries of other parents as the fiery blue spokes of light overran the plain, bounced and careened over the Earth children, engulfed them. Shrieks of agony rose into the crystal night air.

"Karla! Oh God!" Marge's eyes were riveted to the screen where her daughter was seized in blue light, her body rigid and quivering, her hair an electrified blonde halo. Her eyes wide with agony and terror, she mouthed the words Mama Mama. Marge tore herself from Karla's arms and ran.

Karla leaped after her, grasped her shoulders, dragged her back. "There's nothing we can do!"

Clinging to each other, they watched their daughter writhe and twist in the devouring blue flame.

Gradually, slowly, the blue dimmed, faded, died. Julie and all the children near her slumped to the ground, limbs twitching. Then they lay still, utterly motionless.

"She's dead." Karla's voice was toneless. "It didn't work. We killed her. We've killed our children and theirs too."

She released Marge, turned from the sight of the deathly still little figures. The gamble had been lost. Why ever had they risked the one great treasure in their lives?

"No, Karla. Look."

The children were stirring. Soon Julie shook her head, rolled over, sat up, looked at the children around her who were also sitting up and staring at each other and down at themselves. Julie looked at her hands, turned them over and back, examining them. She plucked at her clothing, touched the clothing of the black girl next to her. The black girl stood, took a tentative step, stumbled, kept her balance. Julie got up, facing the mountains, but looking down at her feet — and tumbled to the ground. The black girl reached for Julie's hands, pulled her up. Carefully, Julie placed one foot in front of the other, arms extended for balance. Several minutes later she was walking with grace and ease. She tried a clumsy trot, joined hands with the black girl, and ran in an awkward circle.

Children all around them joined hands, ran back and forth. From the plain rose the treble of children, voices screaming, shrieking with joy.

"Julie," breathed Marge Bowman.

Karla Cooper knelt to her seven-year old daughter, took the small hands in hers and looked into her eyes.

Blue eyes looked back into hers with awareness; they contained what all the doctors, all the neurologists, all the genetics experts had said was forever impossible for their retarded child: intelligence.

Julie Bowman-Cooper spoke. "I know only these Earth words until you teach me more." She spoke in a childish lisp, but without a trace of the speech dysfunction that had always caused her to slur her words. "My natal beings who cherish me wish to thank you."

Marge Bowman lifted her eyes to the spaceship which was rising slowly from the surface of the Earth, on its way back to the lonely stars.

"Thank you," she whispered. "We'll do our very best."

JESSIE

I

"It's a bad time for you to visit, Kate," Sheriff Jessie Graham offered in quiet apology.

"I'm glad to be here, Jess," Kate replied with equal quietness. "I know how close you are to Walt. Right now you need your friends."

Kate Delafield, sipping coffee from a styrofoam cup, sat beside Jessie Graham's desk in one of the plain wooden chairs the county of Alta Vista provided for visitors to its Sheriff's station at Seacliff. She said to Jessie, "As I recall, he helped you get this job."

Jessie nodded. "I owe it to him."

"You say he disappeared Friday. Any theories about why — or where he might be?"

Jessie contemplated Kate Delafield, the strong face framed by fine graying hair, the intelligent, somber light blue eyes. Kate had last stopped here for a visit more than two years ago, and Anne had been with her. Anne's accident, her death, had happened two months after that, and Jessie had not learned of it until a week after the funeral . . .

"Woman, you're on vacation," Jessie growled, reaching to place a hand over Kate's arm, and pointedly surveying Kate's jeans and the hooded white sweatshirt adorned with a small LAPD insignia. "You're not four hours out of that smog-ridden cesspool, I'm not about to — "

"The smog's a little better in L. A. these days, Jess," Kate said with a faint smile. She slouched back into the wooden chair as if it were comfortably cushioned, and crossed an ankle over a knee. She picked up her cup of coffee. "My friend, tell me about it."

"It's a hell of a thing." For the first time in two days Jessie felt the pressure within her ease, felt a sense of comfort. She pushed herself back from her desk, rested a foot on an open desk drawer, folded her arms across her brown uniform shirt. She said in a rush of words, "There's no damn sense to it, Kate, I played cards with the man and four friends of ours Friday night, I swear he was the same as always. He left my place making jokes and waving twenty-seven dollars in winnings, he'd taken most of those dollars from me. The next morning Walt's wife calls me, claims that in the middle of that very same night he'd taken off in pouring down rain with a bag of money under his arm, without his car, and nobody's seen hide nor hair of him since. There's no *sense* to it."

Kate shook her head sympathetically; her eyes narrowed in scrutiny of her friend. "Any theories, Jess?"

"Theoretically," Jessie said with all the confidence she could muster, "he's a missing person, he may just turn up like a lot of them do." Then she felt a stinging behind her eyes and looked quickly away. "Kate — dammit, Kate, I know in my gut he's dead."

When she could control her voice she said almost angrily, "My gut feelings don't always turn out to be fact." She forced a semblance of a grin. "I had a gut feeling about Irene, too. That we'd be together forever."

"I know the feeling." Kate gestured at the case file on Jessie's desk. "Could I take a look?" Jessie handed it over. "Tell me everything, Jess. Everything you've got, right down to the fine hairs."

Jessie nodded gratefully. Then scowled, remembering the Saturday morning two days ago in Walt Kennon's house.

Velma Kennon had been seated in an armchair in the immaculate living room, her red-checked apron clashing violently with the pale lavender of the upholstery. She pulled a grey cardigan loosely around her shoulders and said in soft, reluctant tones, "He had me draw out the ten thousand from our savings Friday."

Jessie's voice was sharp with skepticism. "Why'd he have you do that? Why wouldn't he do it himself?"

"Maybe it was his way of telling me." Her voice broke. "I think he was in some kind of trouble."

If she expects me to fall for this horse manure . . .

"I *know* him," Jessie said. "You're Walt's wife — but it's only been a year for you, Velma." There was hostility in her tone that she had not intended, and she added more gently, "I grew up knowing the man, we've been close friends ever since I came back to Seacliff. I *know* Walt. There's no sense to this."

Velma picked up a corner of her checked apron and dabbed at a cheek. "Well, I thought Walter loved me."

Jessie asked with renewed brusqueness, "What'd Walt say he needed the ten thousand for?"

"He said I should just trust him." The voice throbbed with
injury. "Said he'd explain it all later. I think he needed that
money to pay someone off, I think he was in some kind of
serious trouble. Maybe trouble from back when he was Sheriff
here. And whoever it was took him somewhere and . . . Maybe
the ocean."

Jessie pushed herself to her feet, shifted her hands down
to rest them just above the wide belt and holster. "He'll have
to be missing forty-eight hours before it's official. But I'd like
to have a look around now if it's all right with you, Velma."

Velma uncrossed her thin ankles and rose to her full
height, not much over five feet. Her dark eyes were
reproachful. "I'd never have called you if I didn't want you
looking into this anyway you can. Go right ahead, look
everywhere."

Jessie radioed for a car to pick up Cowan, the deputy who
had accompanied her; she wanted to be alone as she sifted
through the possessions of Walter Kennan. She knew she
might spot something odd, some little thing Cowan could miss.

After Cowan was gone, she sat in her Sheriff's car trying to
collect her thoughts and fight down an almost paralyzing
foreboding. Not for a moment did she believe one detail of
Velma Kennon's story.

In two days of hearings before the seven Commissioners of
Alta Vista County, Jessie had learned all she needed to know
about the character of Walt Kennon. Ten years a retired
Sheriff, he had challenged the Commissioners to ignore
Jessie's superior record, her solid years of experience in police
work in both Los Angeles and Alta Vista County, her
administrative ability, her leadership qualities. Jessie knew that
she owed the position she had held for the past year and a half
entirely to Walt Kennon.

Groping for objectivity, she reviewed the facts she readily
knew about him. He was sixty-four. He'd been released from
Veterans' Hospital in '46, some months after the war. Had

finished his education at Cal Poly in San Luis Obispo, then come back to Seacliff and taken up police work, rising to the position of Sheriff. But the shrapnel fragments still scattered throughout both his legs and the persistent severe pain had led to his early retirement twelve years later. Of his wartime experiences she remembered him saying only, "Duty. Loyalty. A man owes it."

He had settled into the town of his birth just as Jessie had — like a thirsty plant sinking deep roots. And like Jessie, had grumbled at every evidence of the oceanside town's growth. Walt's only vacations had been to Los Angeles to visit a brother afflicted with emphysema, and he returned each time even more contemptuous of big city life. He was Jessie's kind of person: quiet and leather-tough, his friendship a hard won prize, a man who kept to himself until some interior principle signaled him to speak — as he had for Jessie, as he had again just recently when a consortium of builders tried to force re-zoning of a section of mobile homes occupied by elderly residents.

Her mind dark with apprehension, Jessie climbed out of her car and went back into Walt Kennon's house. In the bedroom she inspected Walt's familiar plaid shirts and windbreakers, the baggy corduroys he usually wore around town and to her card games, his khaki gardening pants, the fleece-lined jacket for the few really chill days of winter, the well-worn cardigan sweaters, the one good blue suit with the white shirt protected by plastic. Like herself, Walt had few clothes; he preferred what was tried and true and comfortable. Jessie noted that the clothes Walt had worn last night — gray corduroys, a blue plaid Pendleton shirt, a black plastic raincoat — were not in the closet. Everything there seemed orderly, undisturbed.

As did Velma's closet. The contents were modest: housedresses and cotton robes, a few skirts and frilly blouses, three good woolen dresses. But inside several large zippered plastic bags were smartly styled suits and dinner dresses, high-heeled sandals and evening shoes stored in plastic compartments — all of these apparently relics from Velma's past, and all of them useless in quiet, informal Seacliff.

Jessie was glad to move her scrutiny from the bedroom to an area less evocative of Velma and Walt Kennon's marriage. In the living room, dozens of *Field and Stream* back issues on the inconspicuous bottom shelf of the small bookcase were the only concrete traces of Walt Kennon. In heterosexual marriage, Jessie mused as she browsed around the carefully appointed room, precious little of a house ever really belonged to the male; his part of the closets maybe, and the yard and garage. The living room *always* belonged to the woman. Yet there was no evidence of Velma in this room either, Jessie realized — or anywhere else. Odd that the house had changed so little during the entire year of Walt Kennon's second marriage.

Remembering how swiftly she'd made her own quarters austere again after the three year disaster with Irene in Los Angeles, Jessie moved into the den adjoining the living room. She looked at a framed photo of Velma and Walt on the small, leather-topped desk, and admitted that she disliked Velma Kennon intensely.

And yet she'd accepted her at first, and willingly. Walt had been five years alone with his grief, and it was good to see him happy. And Velma was a pretty woman, and vivacious. But the buoyancy had soon left Walt's step. And Velma's prettiness and high energy seemed to fade with each succeeding month of her marriage to Walt. Only once in the past year had Walt invited the Friday night poker group to his house — when Velma was away visiting her parents in Garden Grove. Walt and Velma seemed to be two people who had leeched the vitality from each other.

Jessie could easily account for Walt's faithfulness to this joyless marriage — the same reason he had never questioned his wartime obligation: *Duty. Loyalty. A man owes it.* As for Velma's reason, it appeared to be the classic one: she had no means of support other than Walt Kennon.

Jessie opened the top drawer of the desk. She found a twenty-five thousand dollar insurance policy, Velma Kennon beneficiary; a copy of a deed to property in Santa Barbara which had been signed over to Bergan Construction Company on January ninth — only two months ago; and a bank book. She opened the bank book. It showed a ten thousand dollar withdrawal made this past Friday and a current balance of two hundred and eighty-six thousand dollars; two hundred and fifty thousand of that amount had been deposited on January nineteenth.

Jessie gaped at the numbers for only an instant. She knew all the surface details of Walt's life, he'd willingly shared them; but never had she heard him speak specifically of his finances. No more than he had ever shared his grief and loneliness for Alice, or talked of how his legs had been shot from under him during the assault on Guadalcanal. He'd muttered about the cost of living — had grumbled at the card game about expensive repairs to his Toyota — but she knew he contributed to the support of his chronically ill brother, and he always seemed to have sufficient money. She had assumed that he lived in relative comfort on a combination of military and police pensions and social security.

"Velma," Jessie called, "could you please come in here a minute?"

Velma glanced blandly at the bank book. "It's Walter's money. His savings, and proceeds from selling a house in Santa Barbara that belonged to his first wife." Her voice took on bitterness. "When my first husband died I didn't have two thin dimes left after probate."

Jessie tapped the bank book with a fingernail. "Says here it's your money as well, Velma. As joint tenant." Then she added reflectively, "I remember about that Santa Barbara house — Alice wouldn't sell it. Amazing it was worth so much money."

"The land it's on was re-zoned commercial years ago. She never did one thing with that place for years," Velma said harshly. "Never even raised the rent of the people living there. Him either, after she died."

"Alice liked the tenants," Jessie said mildly, picking up the executed deed, turning it over in her hands, her mind lighted with the image of Alice Kennon. Genial, comfortable Alice, with mink brown hair that had suddenly gone gray and then whitened over the years, and hazel eyes always radiating humor and spirit, conveying that everything about Jessie — everything — was just fine with her. She had given Walt Kennon a glow of quiet contentment for twenty-six years, until the diagnosis of pancreatic cancer. Just a scant six weeks after that, Jessie Graham had borne one of the heaviest burdens of her life — the casket of Alice Kennon to her gravesite in Rolling Hills Cemetery.

Replacing the documents, Jessie brushed a finger along the lock mechanism on the drawer. She bent down to examine it. "Walt mentioned a couple of weeks ago he'd made out a will, to make sure his brother was taken care of. One of those handwritten wills. Holographic, they call them."

Velma looked startled. "I don't know about any will." She added with belligerence, "I never saw it."

"Drawer's been forced open," Jessie stated, watching her. "You know why that'd be?"

Two thin furrows formed between the penciled brows. "The drawer's never once been locked so far as I know. I don't know what anybody'd take."

Maybe that will.

The yard was neat, well tended, the grass wet and spongy under Jessie's feet. The pain in Walt's legs had limited how much he could do but he loved gardening, and well-cultivated flower beds bordered the front of the house and the side hedge. Last night's heavy rain had separated and caked the dirt around the bushes.

Jessie walked up the driveway past the house and opened the garage. The gray Toyota was parked against one wall; garden utensils lined the opposite wall. A few wood-working tools lay on a scarred bench. She picked up a plastic hood and covered the circular saw that Walt used to cut his firewood. A movement caught her eyes; she glanced over to catch the flutter of curtain at the kitchen window.

So Velma was watching her. With heightened senses she examined the garage minutely, donning a pair of Walt's work gloves to pick up and study each tool. She found nothing unusual until she came to a well-used but very clean shovel. At the kitchen window, Velma Kennon watched openly as Jessie studied it. She replaced the shovel and went into the house.

Velma stood at the kitchen counter slicing a tomato; its rich earthy odor reached Jessie. It occurred to her that she had always seen Velma Kennon in a colorless dress covered by a red-checked apron with big pockets.

Jessie said evenly, "That's a mighty clean shovel out there in the garage."

"Walter left it out in the rain last week," Velma said, her eyes on the knife slicing through the ripe red tomato.

"Didn't rain last week," Jessie informed her.

"Well, whenever it last did," Velma said in exasperation.

Jessie said, not bothering to soften her skepticism, "Being careless with one of his tools isn't something Walt would do."

Velma's knife stilled. She stared at Jessie, then said with asperity, "It doesn't sound like Walter to just go off and disappear without a trace, either."

"Don't think that's what he did."

She locked eyes with Velma Kennon. Velma's unreadable dark stare did not waver. Finally Jessie said, "Could I trouble you for the keys to the Toyota?"

She followed Velma into the living room. Velma picked up her purse from the desk.

"Could I trouble you to look at the purse," Jessie said. "Just routine."

"Of course," Velma said with distinct sarcasm, and thrust the leather bag at Jessie, her fingers rigid. "As I recall, I think I've got thirty-two dollars in bills, and a little change."

Jessie did not reply. Of course Velma wouldn't be stupid enough to carry any of that ten thousand dollars in her purse. Removing one object at a time, she carefully placed on the desk a comb, wallet, lipstick, compact, metal nail file, package of tissues, ballpoint pen, checkbook. The checkbook register showed ordinary transactions.

"The ten thousand," Jessie said. "What denominations did the bank give you?" She examined the zippered pocket and lining of the black leather purse.

"Five hundred in twenties," Velma muttered, her lips in a thin tight line, "the rest in fifties and hundreds."

Jessie nodded. "That's quite a wad of cash." She handed the purse back to Velma. "I'll let you put everything back the way you want. We have to look at everything, Velma. Just routine," she added absently, thinking that Walt had bought chips at the poker game with two tens.

Jessie unlocked the car. The Toyota Celica showed the usual signs of five-year wear, and smelled of Walt's pipe tobacco. She added the powerful beam of her flashlight to the morning sunlight, and examined the interior. She'd impound the car; Elbert and Ron over at Martinsville would go over it thoroughly. But there were no visible stains. Of any kind.

Deep in thought, she walked slowly to her own car and replaced the flashlight in its sprocket. Money and property were the reasons for many marriages — and the motive for the vast majority of crime. Most people would say Velma was not the type to kill, but she knew anybody was the type. Knew it from those years of police work down in Los Angeles and fifty-two years of plain hard living. Only their Maker knew why people did the things they did.

Something had happened to Walt — and Velma had done it. Of that Jessie was certain. She shifted her gunbelt, adjusting the heavy holster, wishing she could do the same for her leaden heart. Velma had done something to him, and taken him somewhere to dispose of him.

But where? And how? It just wasn't physically possible for a hundred and ten pound woman of nearly fifty to do much with a man Walt's size, certainly not against his will, and not if he was dead weight, either. Walt had become heavier recently; he was a good hundred and seventy pounds, maybe more. He'd joked ruefully about it just last night as he helped himself to potato chips and dip at the poker game . . .

Another memory of the poker game leaped into Jessie's mind. She whirled and trotted back to the Toyota. Walt's complaint about expensive repairs to the Toyota — he'd picked up the car on the way to the poker game, he'd had it in for a brake relining and carburetor work, plus routine maintenance . . .

Jessie yanked open the car door, knelt to scan the Union Oil sticker on the door frame, then compared the mileage figure written there by the service station to the mileage on the speedometer, jotting the numbers in her note pad. Velma Kennon watched from the kitchen window.

From the time Walt had picked up the car it had been driven two miles and whatever number of tenths that were unaccounted for. Gil's Union Oil Station was around the corner from the Kennon house; Walt had driven from there to Jessie's house for poker. Based on the time Velma had given as Walt's arrival home, he'd come directly here from the poker game. By marking off those distances in her own car she could tell if Walt's car had been driven after he'd arrived at his house. One thing she knew for sure: If this car *had* been driven, it hadn't been driven far.

Concealing her excitement, Jessie clumped back into the house. "Velma," she asked, "you drive that car after Walt got home last night?"

"Why . . . no. Of course not."

"I'm sealing it off, impounding it for the time being. I'll say goodbye to you for now."

Velma wiped her hands on her checked apron. "Something bad's happened to him," she said. "I know it."

I'll bet you do.

"I guarantee," Jessie said, her tone heavy and ominous, "I'll find out. One way or the other, I'll find out."

She had turned then and stalked out to her police car.

II

Jessie had taken Kate to an early dinner at the Sandpiper, a weathered clapboard restaurant on a steep hillside overlooking Seacliff and the Pacific. She restrained herself from supplying more details of Walt Kennon's disappearance while Kate gazed at a bank of fog drifting its way in over the horizon, over white-capped swells of gray-blue ocean.

"As good a career as you had in L. A.," Kate said musingly, "I can see what compelled you to come back here."

Jessie smiled, and realized that she had not smiled in the past three days. "Much as I don't understand it, Kate, I see that you belong where you are, too. They need the best cops they can find down there in that nether side of hell."

Smiling, Kate picked up her scotch. "You don't get lonely up here, Jess, away from any sort of . . . activity?"

"Gay women, you mean." Jessie refrained from pointing out that Kate herself was on vacation alone. "We do have gay people here — hell, we're everywhere. Seacliff has fourteen thousand population now, it's a fair-sized place. A few folks know about me . . . some of them have long memories. I was chasing after girls in this town from the time I was six."

She chuckled along with Kate. "I'm private about myself just naturally. But I can't say I'm all that careful, even though some people here would jump at any reason to see me gone. They can't abide the idea of a woman Sheriff, let alone — "

Jessie broke off to Kate's raised hand. Their first course, clam chowder, had arrived. Intoxicated by the aroma, Jessie dipped her spoon eagerly into the rich meaty creaminess, realizing that she had scarcely eaten since Saturday. As the waitress moved away Jessie continued, wolfing down the chowder as she spoke, "I'll tell you the truth. My time with Irene told me one thing plain as day — I'm cut out to be a bachelor. I'm still your perfectly normal queer," she added with an embarrassed grin, "I do love women, I drive up to San Francisco now and again and get in some girl chasing. But this town is my family, I've got roots here, and responsibility, good friends — " She broke off and put down her soup spoon. Walt's disappearance was again like an iron weight in her stomach, displacing further desire for food.

"Tell me about the Kennon car." Kate's voice was dry, business-like. "I assume it checked out clean?"

Jessie's smile was inward. Kate had not changed much; when her mind was locked into the details of a case, she spared limited attention for even such distractions as spectacular views of the Pacific or general conversation.

"No traces of blood," Jessie answered, "not in the car or on any of the tools. And Velma was made joint tenant on the savings account the week after Walt married her. Walt's the kind to do something like that."

Kate finished the last spoonful of her chowder, pushed the bowl away. She steepled her fingers and contemplated Jessie over them. "That's a point, Jess. If you're right about your gut feeling then the motive here figures to be money, pure and simple. Since she's joint tenant, why would she do anything to

Walt? Why wouldn't she just clean out that account and take off?"

Jessie nodded. "It's a good point. But I've figured out a couple of reasons. Velma doesn't seem the type to run even if she knew how to cover her tracks, and that's a lot harder to do in these days of computers. She'd have to cover her tracks awfully well with Walt after her, him being an ex-cop. I think she'd figure he'd track her down, she wouldn't feel safe for a minute."

"And if she simply divorced him," Kate mused, "she probably wouldn't come out with much of a settlement, considering the length of their marriage."

Jessie moved her soup bowl aside and pulled a folded sheet from the Kennon case file, a real estate map of Seacliff. "I've measured mileage to the exact tenth, Kate. Drove from Gil's Union Station to my house, then back to Walt's. I've got to think he came as direct as he could to my place — Gil at the station said Walt picked the car up at six fifty-five, five minutes before the station closed. Walt arrived just after seven, like he usually did, and I've got four other witnesses to prove it."

"And afterward," Kate contributed, "aside from Velma's statement about when he arrived home, he wouldn't have reason to go anywhere. It was pouring rain — "

"And everything in town was closed, anyway," Jessie concluded. "So I got one and eight-tenths miles clicked off what Walt drove. That leaves an extra two tenths to account for, plus whatever other tenths were on there because the gas station only wrote down the whole number. Meaning Walt or Velma drove the car half of that distance, and Velma drove it back the other half."

Jessie extracted a pen from her uniform shirt pocket with the ease of habit. "Here's the Kennon house." She indicated a point on the map in the center of a circle inscribed in pencil. "I took a compass and measured and drew this circle around the Kennon house — "

Kate reached for the map, studied it closely. Jessie said, "Most of it's residential."

"True," Kate said, "but there's some vacant land in here, Jess, and part of a cemetery."

"Rolling Hills Cemetery," Jessie said with a nod. "Alice Kennon's buried just on the other side of my circle. The cemetery's all grass, kept perfect, just like a lawn, I checked it out Sunday. And all that vacant land, I walked every bit of it, Kate. I looked at every damn square inch."

"You said it rained hard Friday night," Kate pointed out. "Heavy rain could cover up traces of a grave."

Jessie looked at her soberly. "I'll tell you the truth. I don't expect to find a grave. I mean, how could a little thing like Velma Kennon dig a grave? Anybody who's ever put a shovel into the ground can tell you uncultivated earth is like digging into cement. Earth wet from rain is like lifting a pile of rocks."

Their food arrived. Jessie looked at her swordfish with indifference. Kate sprinkled lemon on her lobster, then cut off a piece and munched on it as she continued her study of the real estate map.

Jessie said, "Let me fill you in about the other leads I checked out."

"Sheriff Graham," the young teller had said nervously, "I gave Mrs. Kennon just what she asked for — "

"I know you did, Sarah. Now just relax," Jessie said in her most reassuring tones. "There's no problem about it at all. Were any of the bills in series?"

Sarah nodded. "But that much money in cash, I had to take it from the PG&E payroll, and that's close onto a hundred fifty thousand dollars, so there's no telling which of those bills I gave her."

Disappointed, Jessie said, "Thank you, Sarah. You call me now if you see any transaction Mrs. Kennon makes that's unusual, all right? Confidential, you have my word."

Jessie interviewed Ms. Neville, the librarian, who had telephoned Saturday afternoon as word of Walter Kennon's disappearance spread around town.

"It was six weeks ago, Sheriff." Ms. Neville peered at Jessie over the narrow rectangles of her reading glasses. "She never did check anything out. Every day for a week she came in here. And hasn't been back since." Her words were a sibilant, penetrating whisper in the single-room cavern that was Seacliff's public library, crowded and murmurous at this mid-afternoon hour on the weekend. "Can't say what she was reading, either. And that's what seemed so suspicious. She'd just put her book right back up on the shelf and move off if I came anywhere near."

The librarian's reproachful frown deepened. "Why would anybody care if another person saw what she was reading?"

Maybe she just flat resented your nosiness, Jessie thought. But she said gently, "Ms. Neville, can you tell me what general section she spent her time in?"

"The sciences. Anatomy. Medicine."

Jessie cut several pieces from her swordfish, moved them around on her plate. "I'll tell you what else I did. I talked to everybody in the Kennon neighborhood — nothing. I ran a check on Velma Kennon's background — nothing. I sent urgent inquiries to every doctor and pharmacy in Alta Vista county, all I've turned up so far is a Darvon prescription when Walt had dental surgery."

Jessie took a forkful of baked potato. "I'll tell you, Kate, I'm baffled. I can't figure what Velma did or how she did it. Right now my theory . . . " She thrust the forkful of potato down in recoil from the images. "I think maybe she's chopped him up and got a piece tucked here and there." She braced, expecting incredulous laughter.

But Kate said firmly, "Jess, put that nightmare out of your head. I'm not claiming this woman doesn't have the alligator mentality it takes to do such a thing, we both know better. But look at your own body, think about all those quarts of blood. Imagine anybody trying to cut through bone and muscle. Imagine the kidneys, the intestines. With all respect, Jess — "

Jessie nodded hurriedly, feeling both foolish and immensely relieved. "Got to be an answer to this, Kate. Got to be."

Kate said, "Why don't I take a few bites of that swordfish you don't want?"

Jessie cut a large section from her fish. "The rest of this'll be a nice treat for Damon, my cat."

Kate nodded absently, her eyes once more on the Pacific. "Before we go to your place, I'd like you to drive me around the circle on this map. While it's still light."

III

Velma Kennon sat in her living room sipping tea, the day's *Courier* in her lap. But she was watching the patrol car, a black menace drifting along her street. Having passed the house twice, it would circle the block and come back once more. And a half hour from now, repeat the process. Velma knew the habits of Seacliff's Sheriff's Department well; she had been under its close surveillance for the past three days.

With an irritated shrug she unfolded the *Courier*. Her eyes were instantly drawn by a name in a small headline down the page:

Former D.A.R. Chapter Pres.
Margaret Paxton Dies Here

She shook the paper open and scanned the short article extolling the accomplishments of Margaret Paxton, sister to the recently deceased Grant Paxton, then turned to the obituary page. The notice was almost identical to the one six days ago which had branded itself into her memory. Chilled, she dropped the paper back into her lap, stared out at the black police car cruising back past the house.

Not much longer, she reassured herself, sipping the hot, bracing tea. Only a matter of days before Sheriff Jessie Graham could no longer justify detaining her in Seacliff, before the Sheriff would have to pursue her all the way to the coast of Florida if she wanted to continue her useless surveillance. A few years from now Velma Gardiner Kennon would be the stuff of memory and legend in this town, the suspected murderess who had somehow conjured away the body of her husband.

Soon . . . it would all happen soon, and exactly as she'd planned. She had a nice solid nest egg now, and the day would come when she'd have even more — when Walter was declared dead and his life insurance paid off, and the title to the house would clear as well. A few more days and she'd have her freedom. After two years of pure misery, she'd earned it.

Never again would she suffer the humiliation of facing the future without resources. She would be able to forget those months of paralysis after Johnny's heart attack and the stunning news of his insolvency, when all the security she'd taken for granted for nearly thirty years had been wiped out. And the bitter months afterward when she'd been forced to live on the proceeds from her few good pieces of jewelry, when she'd learned how friendships just melted away once you were in trouble. And the job she'd been forced to accept as cashier in the dining room of The Duquesne, a hotel frequented by traveling salesmen and the women who found its dining room and bar convenient for assignations with those salesmen.

Walter Kennon had been an anomaly in such surroundings, pure chance bringing him there for the ten days of his visit with his ill brother. His interest in her had been tentative, shy and awkward; and she, having by this time taken cold-eyed stock of her situation, knew that marrying a man like the colorless, uninteresting Walter Kennon was probably about as well as she could do.

When he said she resembled his deeply mourned Alice, she had laid siege to Walter Kennon's affections by asking myriad questions about Alice, then pretending to be like her in every way she could devise. To her despair, Walter had returned to Seacliff after those ten days — but a month later reappeared to sheepishly propose marriage. That very same day she had resigned her detested job and, in triumph, traveled back with him to Seacliff.

But the town was slow-paced and quiet beyond all imagining. The spring and summer months of cloudy, foggy weather were depressing, unmitigated by the presence of the ocean; and the modest stucco or frame houses and their ordinary inhabitants were equally depressing. Her first husband had loved to socialize, to dance and drink; Walter Kennon sternly disapproved of alcohol, and looked forward only to his weekly poker game. Of all her pretense before their marriage, he was most unforgiving of the lie that she, like Alice, knew the game of poker and loved to play it.

But, deadly dull as Walter Kennon might be, he was, she conceded, kind and decent, and a good provider. She lived comfortably, if not agreeably.

In the first days of their marriage he had shown her the contents of the locked desk drawer. "So you can rest easy about everything," he told her. "There'll be plenty enough for you, but I've written out this will making it a condition my brother Ralph's taken care of, too. I've made Jessie Graham executor, I'm depending on you both."

She had agreed, of course. She seldom disagreed, argued even more rarely. As the waif taken under his wing, any wishes of hers were subordinate to his decisions, and in his house she could not so much as move a pillow from sofa to chair without him moving it back. The ghost of Alice Kennon pervaded every room including the bedroom: Walter was indifferent to her physically.

Every aspect of their marriage was a sham; and her status in the life of this man, her distinct inferior, added a fresh layer of gall to all her other humiliations. Walter Kennon had married her only to keep his memories alive, to serve as a reflection of his enshrined Alice.

Smothered by her life, without any acceptable alternative, she daydreamed of moving back to Los Angeles to flaunt economic independence under the noses of the "friends" who had deserted her; she yearned to live independently amid the bright lights and energy of a major city. She longed for freedom unencumbered by Walter Kennon.

Then the letter from Bergan Construction Company had arrived. The company was interested in the property in Santa Barbara, prepared to make an offer. There was a toll-free eight-hundred number to call.

Walter had crumpled the letter, thrown it into the trash. "Alice's parents left her that house. The Herreras, they've lived there for years, Alice promised they could stay so long as they pay the taxes and upkeep on the place. I'm bound to keep that promise."

She had fished out the letter and called the toll-free number the following day. And learned that the land was now re-zoned, and Bergan Construction would offer a quarter of a million dollars clear cash, the buyer paying all expenses of the sale. Stunned by the magnitude of the offer, she explained the situation. Perhaps, Jack Bergan suggested, with Mrs. Kennon's

approval, and provided he had her cooperation in the matter
of selling the property to him, he himself might talk to the
tenants. Perhaps they could be persuaded to move out on their
own . . .

Two weeks later a terse communication had arrived from
Mr. and Mrs. Raul Herrera. At the end of the month they
would be vacating the home they had lived in for nearly thirty
years. The brevity of the note, its coldness, had bewildered,
then hurt, then infuriated Walter.

At the height of his railing over the Herraras' lack of
gratitude, Velma detailed the problems involved in
refurbishing the house and finding suitable new tenants. When
another letter from Jack Bergan fortuitously arrived in the
next day's mail, Walter picked up the phone and called the
eight-hundred number. Velma did not know how Jack Bergan
had managed the Herreras' eviction, nor did she ever inquire.

She was now joint tenant on a bank account amounting to
over two hundred and ninety thousand dollars, and heir to the
house and Walter's life insurance and pensions besides. She
could not simply take the money from the bank account —
even if Walter's friends at the bank did not notify him
moments after such a withdrawal, where could she run to that
Walter would not find her? No, it would all be hers only when
Walter died, and never mind that blood-sucking brother of his.

If only Walter would die.

The phrase echoing in her mind, she immediately told
herself she meant nothing by it. Over the following days, as the
thought further implanted itself, she argued that she was not
truly contemplating murder, merely examining the possibility
out of pure curiosity. And she continued to repeat this to
herself during the months she spent seeking a method, a
foolproof plan: she was merely searching out the solution to a
difficult and fascinating puzzle, the only interesting thing she'd
found to do since coming to this dreary town.

It was no easy matter, she learned, to safely rid oneself of a person. Modern crime detection techniques were too highly sophisticated. And when the person was an ex-Sheriff who knew how to protect himself, who had strong ties to current law enforcement, the problem was immeasurably more thorny.

She dismissed the idea of a handgun: how did one go about finding an unregistered weapon and disposing of it properly afterward? Walter of course had a gun — his old service revolver — but the possibility of arranging an accident with that weapon seemed hopeless.

And how did one go about obtaining undetectable or untraceable poison? Stabbing was out of the question; it required expertise as well as a high degree of luck, and made a dreadful mess besides. Other methods — gassing, bludgeoning, pushing Walter from a height, arranging an accident with the car — presented their own problems. What if the result was not death but permanent injury? What could be worse than being condemned to caring for Walter Kennon, invalid, for the rest of her life or his? And if she was caught and convicted of murder, she would undoubtedly go to jail for the rest of her life, if not face a hideous death inhaling cyanide in California's gas chamber.

Given the fact that any method had to be absolutely foolproof, arranging Walter's death by other than natural causes seemed an impossibility. Yet there had to be some way . . .

IV

As Jessie traversed the circle she had drawn on the real estate map, Kate asked several times to stop. Once she got out of the car to look over a low bluff into a grassy ravine; then to tramp a weed-choked lot; then to scuff a jogging shoe in the dirt of another lot recently cleared of its brush. As daylight faded to gray, she had Jessie stop at Rolling Hills Cemetery.

Jessie stood with Kate on the tar-surfaced road alongside the graveyard, its long green hillside extending all the way down to the fog-shrouded sea perhaps a quarter of a mile away. A hand extended over her eyes as if she were shading them from the sun, Kate looked out over the perfectly sodded graves with their imbedded granite markers.

Realizing the memories undoubtedly triggered by this scene, Jessie offered gruffly, "My folks are buried here, you know." She gestured toward a distant green hill. "On the old side where Alice Kennon is. It doesn't have these flat headstones that all look alike." As Kate nodded in reply, Jessie reflected that she herself was getting just as cantankerous as Walt Kennon about every change in the world she knew and loved.

Kate lowered herself to a knee and ran a hand over the bent Bermuda grass of the hillside. "Tell me again what Walt was wearing Friday night."

"Gray corduroys, a blue plaid Pendleton shirt."

"A plastic raincoat, you said."

"That too. He arrived in it, left in it. A black one."

Kate stood, brushed her hands together to remove the dust of the grass. She walked slowly and for some distance along the hillside, stopping just beyond a white stake to examine a single tire track beside the paved road, any distinguishing features of the track obliterated by the recent rain.

"I have to tell you," Jessie muttered, staring down the smooth, steep hillside, "I considered the notion Velma might've rolled him down this hill and all the way to the ocean, I really did. I even walked it. But the land flattens out down there — " She gestured, " — a good hundred yards at the bottom of the hill. No way she could push or drag him to where the hill drops again. No way in hell."

Kate said, "I'd have considered the exact same idea, Jess."

Her hand once more across her eyes, Kate again surveyed the cemetery, a deepening gray shadow as nightfall approached. Jessie felt a renewed comfort that Kate was here and reviewing every detail of this investigation with her.

"Jess."

Alerted by the tone, Jessie looked sharply at Kate; but she was turned away from her.

"Anne told me once she wanted cremation." The tone was low, distant. "But I buried her, you know. Cremation was what her family wanted too, but they were good enough to leave me alone about it. The thing was, she burned to death. I couldn't bear to burn her again. Can you understand that?"

Jessie managed to find her voice. "I do understand. I do."

"But I think about her all the time there in the ground. And her not wanting to be where she is."

Jessie took Kate's arm. "I think she'd want exactly what you wanted," she said quietly, firmly. "I think she'd understand. I think she wouldn't mind."

Kate turned to Jessie, slid an arm around her waist, walked with Jessie toward the police car.

V

Velma could not remember the precise moment when she made the clear and irrevocable decision to kill Walter, but it was soon after that morning when she waited in the car as Walter paid his weekly visit to Alice's grave. She observed the cemetery custodians rolling a freshly sodded grave, completing the interment process for a funeral held the day before, and she realized then that the true key lay not in foolproof method but in foolproof disposal of the body.

In the days afterward she deduced a method for ending
Walter's life that would leave no evidence behind, deduced the
exact circumstances that would allow her to handle more than
a hundred and seventy pounds of dead weight. She decided
that she would roil the waters of an investigation by
withdrawing ten thousand dollars — any lesser amount
seeming insufficient to confuse the issue of Walter's
disappearance — and stash the money under the flower beds
where it could remain until safe to remove; and if it was
discovered in the meantime, what did that prove?

To validate her choice of weapon she made several trips to
the library. Then she carefully fashioned her disposable,
untraceable bludgeon from sand mixed with heavy steel bolts
she found in Walter's tool chest, packing the material into one
of Walter's thick wool socks until she was satisfied with the
weight and heft. Knowing the act itself would take every ounce
of strength, her every fibre of nerve, she waited in a state of
feverish dread for ideal conditions.

Each morning she wrenched open the *Courier* to the
obituary page. Over a period of the next five weeks there were
seven burials at Rolling Hills — but either they were in the old
section of the cemetery, or the weather was clear. Twelve
times it rained — but there was no funeral.

Each morning as Walter ate his breakfast and prepared for
a new day of golf or fishing or gardening, her anxiety grew. It
was now March, and the prime rainy season along the Pacific
coast was waning. She might very well have to wait until late in
the year before the rains returned — six more months at least
of living with Walter in this dismal town before she had a likely
opportunity.

Then she rose on a Friday morning to gathering black
clouds over the ocean and a forecast of rain, occasionally
heavy, throughout the day and night. She pulled from her
apron pocket a two day old obituary:

GRANT R. PAXTON, 68, beloved husband of
Margaret Paxton; loving father of John and Edward
Paxton; devoted grandfather of Christopher and Julie
Paxton. Services Friday, Mar. 7, 11:00 am at First
Presbyterian Church; internment at Rolling Hills
Cemetery.

She had already checked out the Paxton plot; it was
located near the cemetery road and held two Paxtons already,
with room for four more. Best of all, tonight was poker night;
she would not need a pretext to lure Walter to the car at a late
hour. Fearful as she was, just as well he would not be home
until that late hour.

Pacing the living room, she heard his car pull into the
detached garage just before midnight. She flung a raincoat
over her shoulders and dashed from the house, her heart
thudding, a hand clutching the crude truncheon weighting
down her apron pocket.

Walter, his black plastic raincoat shiny with rain, emerged
from the car and blinked at her in surprise.

Her voice raspy with strain, she gasped, "I just noticed I
lost the diamond in my ring. I'm positive it's in the back of the
car."

With a muffled exclamation he turned and yanked open
the rear door. Her heart hammering against her ribs, she
pushed the raincoat from her shoulders and stepped swiftly up
beside him. Gripping the weapon in both hands she swung it
behind her to give it the widest possible arc.

He bent down to climb into the car, then started to rise.
"The car's been at Phil's station. How — "

She hit him squarely and with all of her strength just along
the side and toward the back of the head, exactly where the
medical and anatomy books said it was most dangerous to
sustain a heavy blow.

There was a single sound from him, a grunted expulsion;
then he pitched forward onto the back seat.

She stared, appalled at the concavity in his head, the gray matted hair welling with blood. What had she done wrong? There shouldn't be any blood — there *couldn't* be any stains on the car's upholstery. Panic-stricken, she stuffed the weapon into her apron pocket, hastily untied the apron and climbed over Walter's back to roughly, tightly bind his head.

She felt for the pulse in his wrist, his neck, as the books had said, as she'd practiced on herself. A second blow would not be necessary; there was no pulse. And she could see that the apron had staunched any flow of blood. Calmer now, she climbed out of the car and went around to the other door. Gripping his shoulders, she pulled and tugged at him, sliding him across the seat on his slick plastic raincoat until he was fully in the car. She closed both doors and retrieved her raincoat, and prepared for the rest of what needed to be done.

VI

Hands in the back pockets of her jeans, Kate stared out the huge windows of Jessie's living room, across the redwood deck at the fog-shrouded lights strung out along the ocean shoreline. As Barbra Streisand sang from Jessie's tape player, Kate prowled the room, looking over the record and tape collection, the bookshelves, poking at the fire, looking at the books again.

"Woman, what's bugging you," Jessie growled. "Sit down and relax, you're making Damon nervous." The marmalade-colored cat in her lap was stirring, its ears pricked.

Kate obediently lowered herself into the armchair beside the fire, picked up her scotch. "You sure I can't get you something, Jess?" She gestured to the wicker wine rack against the dining room wall. "You've got some nice reds over there."

Jessie shook her head. "Haven't had a thing to drink since this all began. It's enough trouble as it is to keep my head clear. I'm so tired, a glass of wine would put me out like a light."

"How about some coffee?" Kate's tone was solicitous. "Be glad to make it for you."

"Nope, that'll keep me wide awake and I hope to sleep a few hours tonight." She looked sharply at Kate, who was fidgeting with her scotch. She reiterated, "What's bugging you, woman?"

"Jess . . . " Kate put the scotch down on her coaster.

It was the same quiet use of her name as at the cemetery, and Jessie watched her uneasily.

"There was a funeral last week at Rolling Hills Cemetery," Kate said. It was a statement, not a question.

"Probably," Jessie answered, a prickling sensation along the back of her neck. "There's usually about one a week. I know for sure they buried Grant Paxton there. He ran Seacliff Realty, I knew him to say hello to."

"He was buried last Friday," Kate stated.

Jessie stared at her. "I don't know about that, but I can check it in a second."

She pulled herself out of her leather recliner and moved to the stack of papers on the brick hearth. "I haven't looked at a newspaper in days . . . " She sorted through the stack until she found last Friday's *Courier,* opened it to the obituary page.

Jessie dropped the paper back onto the stack, sat down on the hearth and looked up at Kate. Her hands, all of her flesh was cold. "Like you said, Paxton was buried Friday. What are you telling me, Kate?"

Kate closed her eyes. "I'm sorry, Jess. Your gut feeling about Walter . . . is right."

Jessie rubbed her arms, edged closer to the fire. "I knew it." But still she had hoped . . .

"I'm sorry, Jess," Kate repeated.

"It's better I know. Just tell me how this was done."

VII

Driving slowly through the sheeting windblown rain, Velma pulled onto the road above Rolling Hills Cemetery and extinguished the car lights. The night was opaque in its blackness; and she drifted the car along until the fourth white roadside marker loomed by her side window. She pulled carefully over onto the grassy side of the road just beyond the marker and turned off the engine. She stripped off her raincoat; it would be useless in this downpour, and encumbering. She got out, opened the rear door of the Toyota.

Pulling, tugging Walter by his shoulders, her foot braced against the side of the car, she inched him across the seat until his head emerged from the car and struck the grass. Quickly she climbed into the car behind him and pushed his legs until he pitched fully out.

She closed the car doors, got the shovel out of the trunk. Again she pulled and tugged at Walter until he lay sideways on the hill. Bracing herself once more, she gave his body a mighty shove. He tumbled down the slope, his head flopping; she lost sight of him in the rain-filled blackness.

Carrying the shovel, wiping the pelting rain from her eyes, she staggered down the steep hill and nearly stumbled over his body. She slid the shovel down the hill knowing she could find it later, then pushed Walter, rolling him over and over in the spongy Bermuda grass, the apron coming off his head.

Standing between his legs as if she were pulling a plow, she dragged him farther, the wet slippery grass and Walter's slick plastic raincoat enabling her to maneuver him, as she had judged they would. She and her mother had once used a similar method — a quilt under a huge heavy chest to move it down into the basement. But she had been so much younger then . . .

Rain streaming from her hair into her blind eyes, she moaned with her straining effort. Would she ever get there? Then she tripped over the edge of the tarpaulin and pitched headlong onto the mound of the newly dug Paxton grave.

She sat on the tarpaulin and rested a few moments, her chest heaving. Then she climbed to her feet and used her tiny flashlight to locate the shovel as well as the apron which had come off Walter's head. She removed the rock-weighted tarpaulin, then the freshly laid strips of sod over Grant Paxton's grave, placing the strips with care on the tarpaulin to keep them intact.

Frenziedly, she began to dig, throwing shovel after shovel of the loose dirt onto the tarpaulin; the earth was becoming heavier as the teeming rain soaked it. When she reached a depth of several feet, she turned quickly to Walter.

Gritting her teeth, her arms quivering with the effort, she tugged and maneuvered him to the edge of the grave. Then gave him one final push. He thudded into the grave, face down. She threw in the apron, the weapon still in its pocket, and Walter's car keys.

She shoveled the earth back, grunting with the heaviness of each shovelful, her entire body trembling with this final exertion, and reshaped the mass of it into a mound, the surface a rapidly smoothing mud. Then she lay the strips of sod back. and reset the tarpaulin. And the rocks weighting the corners of the tarpaulin. Then she shook the muddy earth from the shovel, wiped it on grass.

Her legs giving way, her limbs jerking, she collapsed on the hillside in an agony of exhaustion, thinking she might die here herself. The rain picked up in fury, pelting her mercilessly, and she lay unmoving, allowing it to slash the mud from her hands, her feet and legs, her clothes, her face.

As strength seeped back into her, she reviewed her next steps — no time now to make the slightest mistake. She would drive home, change into dry clothes. Destroy Walter's handwritten will in the fireplace and pulverize the ashes —

Abruptly she sat up. She had already made a mistake. The key to the desk was on Walter's keychain; she had buried it along with Walter. She lay back down again. It wasn't that much of a mistake. A sturdy kitchen knife would be sufficient to spring the desk drawer. After taking this much risk she *definitely* would not share any of her gains with anyone. It was now nearly one o'clock; at two she would call the Sheriff's office and report Walter missing, and then it would all be finished.

When her limbs finally ceased their trembling she struggled to her feet and switched on the small flashlight and inspected her handiwork. The Paxton grave looked untouched, the thundering rain continuing to wash away all traces of her presence. Even the shovel had been scoured clean of its evidence. Finally she summoned strength for the climb up the hill to the car, and to freedom. She had done it. And no one could possibly guess how.

VIII

Jessie moved away from the fire. She was warm, heated by anger, her mind seething with the image of the false grief on Velma Kennon's face that Saturday morning, scant hours after Velma had ruthlessly killed her own husband and Jessie's irreplaceable friend.

"I'm sorry," Kate said softly. "There was no good or gentle way to tell you any of this."

No one, Jessie thought, could have been more gentle than Kate. Not even Irene would be as good with her as this woman, with whom she shared an alien profession whose daily stock in trade was violence, who had herself been touched by the annihilating hand of death.

Kate said, "Of course you won't know if I'm right until . . . "

"I know it now." Jessie took a deep breath. "Everything you've theorized makes perfect sense. It does. To do what she did and then put him in someone else's grave — " She hissed, "It's *obscene*."

Kate murmured, "Maybe I can get you some of that wine now?"

Jessie shook her head. She walked over to Kate, sat down on the ottoman in front of her armchair. "I can't imagine how you figured this out."

"Anne told me," Kate said.

Jessie gaped at her.

"And then you told me the rest. The answers all came at Rolling Hills." Kate's eyes were fixed unseeingly on the fire; her voice was remote. "Looking over that place, I was remembering the day after Anne was buried. I drove out to the cemetery very early that next morning. I wanted to be with her . . . I wanted to dig with my bare hands till I could be in there with her . . . . "

Jessie, her eyes stinging, kept her silence. Kate's renewed anguish over Anne was her fault. In sharing Jessie's sorrow, Kate had ripped the scar tissue from her own grief . . .

Kate's voice strengthened. "But you're the one who's responsible for solving this crime. How many investigating officers would have thought to check that Union Oil sticker? Velma Kennon would have gotten away with murder except for you. And your notion about Velma rolling him down the hill and all the way to the ocean — when I realized she wouldn't have to roll him far at all, it came together then, how a new grave as soon as it's rolled and sodded looks just like any other grave. And how Velma could use the rain, the slope of the cemetery and its bent Bermuda grass, Walt's slippery raincoat — " Fixing her somber eyes on Jessie, Kate shrugged. "And aside from all that, it seems after thirteen years in the cop business I'm beginning to think right along with the criminals."

Jessie sighed. She said softly, "You'd best get on to bed, Kate. Much as I want to, I can't lock Velma up tonight — not a thing to be done till morning and I get the search warrant to go in and get Walt. You've got only these few days of vacation, I want you out of here bright and early — "

"I'll stay up with you," Kate said firmly.

Jessie shook her head. "It's all on my shoulders now, Kate. I'd like to be alone with my thoughts."

Kate said quietly, "I do understand that, Jess."

With Kate settled in the guest bedroom, Jessie sat in her armchair and stared into the fire. But she did not yet think of Walt Kennon, or begin to mourn him; there was time enough for that. Instead she thought about Kate Delafield on vacation, making her solitary, lonely way up the California coast.

IX

The next morning, Velma again looked at the *Courier's* obituary page. Margaret Paxton would be buried today next to her dead husband — and Velma's. Velma swallowed the last of her tea and dismissed a brief impulse to attend. That would be foolish, would only arouse comment, if not suspicion. She had not realized that the bond of friendship between Walter Kennon and Jessie Graham ran as deep as it did — and she could not be too careful in these final days of the Sheriff's investigation.

Velma looked up, to see a patrol car coming up the block toward her house. Odd. This was out of pattern — another patrol car had already performed its half-hourly surveillance routine only fifteen minutes ago.

Then the patrol car was joined by Jessie Graham's car with its gold Sheriff's insignia. With a surge of alarm Velma watched both cars turn into her driveway as yet another police car came from the opposite direction to join them, screeching to a stop in front of the house.

Feeling the blood drain from her face, Velma watched Jessie Graham climb out of her car and adjust the gunbelt over her dark brown trousers. The Sheriff reached into her car to retrieve some sort of plastic sack; then marched toward the house at a purposeful pace, flanked by three deputies who drew their weapons as they approached the door.

What could this be? What had gone wrong? She had made no mistakes, *nothing* had gone wrong, there was no way on earth Jessie Graham could know *anything*.

Harassment, she decided. A last-ditch, desperation attempt to panic her, stampede her into making a mistake. Seeing the neighbors gather on their lawns and sidewalks to observe, Velma angrily threw open her front door. "What's the meaning of this . . . *circus?*"

"You're under arrest, Velma." The words were said with barely controlled rage; the dark eyes were implacably cold.

Holding the plastic sack by a corner, Sheriff Jessie Graham held it up to Velma's eyes.

A hand at her throat as if cyanide fumes were already choking her, Velma stared at her dirty, blood-stained apron.

BENNY'S PLACE

Depositing a sack filled with takeout food and a quart of bourbon, Benny stretched out on the army blanket that covered his air mattress. He wasn't hungry yet; and his heart was still pounding.

In the murk of his hideaway he broke the seal on the bourbon and raised his head to take a deep swallow. Throat and eyes burning, he screwed the cap back on and placed the bottle beside him. With a mutter of satisfaction he lay back, hands behind his head, and listened to the rising buzz of voices outside the house.

He was safe. But his precious knife was gone forever. He mourned his loss — the bone handle with the smooth ridges and curves that had fit so well in his fingers and against his

palm, the sharp, gleaming blade. So many hours he'd practiced
in front of a mirror with that knife. Dancing, twisting,
pirouetting . . .

He crossed his ankles and consoled himself by
contemplating his immaculate red and gray Puma jogging
shoes. They, more than his knife, were his stock in trade; he'd
used the knife only once in a while, and for specific purpose.
He'd chosen these shoes carefully, as a craftsman would
choose his tools, and they had yet to fail him. Benny the jag, his
envious friends called him, likening him to the stealthy jaguar
that sped through the jungle with supreme menace. Puma
shoes were perfect for Benny the jag . . .

Treading as softly as a cat, he would glide up behind the
prey he had singled out, and then strike: pull a purse off an
arm or snatch it from a hand. And then he would be gone,
vanishing on his swift silent shoes into the labyrinth of Eastside
Detroit even before the shrieks rose from the woman he had
hurled to the pavement.

Women were his only prey. Women were infinitely,
variously rewarding; he stalked them with the alert instincts
and appetites of his jungle namesake, relishing their shrieks of
alarm, of fear. Periodically, he flicked open his bone-handled
knife and backed one of them into an alley. An old woman
usually — she would be too frail, too terrified to resist, her
eyes wide and staring, jaw working soundlessly with the cold
steel of his knife at her throat.

"Open that ugly mouth, I'm gonna cut you," he would
grate, dexterously wielding his weapon. The greater her terror,
then her horror, the greater his ecstasy. Afterward, he would
race down the alley, vaulting over fences and hedges in
effortless escape.

Now his magical knife, his talisman, was gone; and he
grieved over his loss.

He tensed reflexively at the sound of approaching sirens,
then relaxed, gloating with the certainty of his safety as the

wailing cut off outside the house. From the side yard, more
voices came to his knowing ear, low and masculine at first,
then feminine, uttering moans of shock. Then the masculine
voices gained ascendancy — authoritative, issuing commands.

It was easy to imagine the scene. All the neighbors
gathered like nosy birds around the body. Cops ordering them
away, roping off the area. Just like TV.

Leaning on an elbow, he reached into his sack for a
foam-boxed beef sandwich, grinning as he listened to the
activity.

His mother and Janey arrived; he knew well the explosive
putt-putt of the ancient Volkswagen Beetle which his mother
had driven for as long as he could remember. He could hear no
words, only the rising cadence of Janey's voice; and then his
mother's shriek that dissolved into gulping sobs. Discomfited,
he put down his sandwich.

If they'd just been home like he expected. It was early
Saturday morning, after all — he had a right to expect her and
Janey to be there. Was it his fault they'd had company in the
house?

With the yellow Beetle gone, he'd proceeded to let himself
in the way he always had, loosening the soft putty around the
back basement window pane with his knife, reaching in to
unlatch the window, then carefully replacing the pane, patting
the putty back into place.

Then the hand had fallen on his shoulder.

Only because the knife was in his hand had he done it.
Wheeled and sunk the knife in to the hilt at the same instant
he heard the voice utter "Benny," at the same instant he
recognized his cousin Frank.

In the next seconds Frank clutched at him, then at the
bone handle, blood spurting over his hands as he clawed at his
stomach. He staggered across the yard and to the driveway,
screaming his agony, then collapsing, blood bubbling from his

mouth. Fat Mrs. Harris from across the alley had opened her back door — and slammed it shut.

He had run back to the basement window and opened it, dropped onto the basement floor clutching his sack of food and liquor, closed and latched the window, then climbed the stairs leading to the kitchen. And had raced for safety . . .

Finished with his sandwich, he threw the scraps aside, grinning at the thought of again frustrating his mother's unrelenting war against insects and rodents. He took another pull at his bourbon. He longed to light up a joint, but knew very well how the smell would spread, carried along by airy drafts in the furnace ducts. When he was ten, had first smoked in this place, his mother's footsteps had been a frantic staccato on the hardwood floors, her shouts frustrated fury: "Janey, Janey, *where's* that cursed smell coming from!"

Two cops were talking to his mother in the living room. One, he realized with disgust, was a woman. From long practice he easily picked out the voices carried by the furnace duct that ran close by and warmed his place during the winter months.

"I don't know," his mother said, her voice a low dullness of shame. "I don't see him all that often. Four months ago the last time, and only a few minutes then. The military police, they were watching and almost caught him. He joined the Army, you see, it was the best thing he could do but then he ran away from boot camp — "

He glared into the darkness of his place. That whole Army shit, none of it was his fault. Sure he joined up, but nobody told him how those Army bastards would be snarling at him, ordering him around . . .

"He ran away," his mother repeated. He could imagine her helpless shrug. "And hitchhiked back here a few weeks later. The Army's still looking for him I imagine. When he came here that last time, they came right in after him, you see. But he got away . . . somehow."

He covered his mouth with his T-shirt sleeve to smother his laughter, and took another pull of his bourbon.

He'd found the place just after he turned nine. In a futile attempt to escape a strapping from Janey, he'd run into his bedroom, hidden in his closet.

"Stay in there ye devil!" Janey had bellowed from the bedroom door in her high Irish tenor. "Your mother and me, we'll tend to dinner, then I'll be tending to you!"

Resigned to his punishment, he had morosely sneaked to the bathroom and back to his closet with a glass of water, careful not to creak the floorboards. Then he had knocked over the water. But instead of becoming a spreading mess, the liquid had disappeared down a crack in the wood. He heard a metallic thrumming close below, then dripping. Feeling along the floorboards, he discovered a ridge — but could not raise it up.

He remembered then that his father, before he took off, had always claimed this old house to be a link in the Underground Railroad before the Civil War, that escaping slaves had been hidden away within these very walls. But wherever the slaves were hidden had been torn down and built over.

In wild suspicion and hope, using the heavy jackknife he had stolen from Billy O'Keefe, given impetus by Janey's usual rumbled after-dinner compliment to his mother and the sound of chairs scraping back from the kitchen table, he pried at the ridge, working it loose. Seconds before Janey entered the bedroom, he had pulled the cunningly carpentered trapdoor down after him.

Examining his surroundings, he listened in delight to the confoundment of his mother and Janey as they searched for him. The tiny chamber was shoulder high and a bit wider than a twin bed, its darkness relieved by faint slivers of light admitted through the cracks in the floorboards of his bedroom. A badly rusted kerosene lamp gave evidence of slave days.

He immediately loved the close dark warmth, the feeling of utter safety and secrecy. He minded not at all his companions, creatures which scuttled in panic from his superior presence. Later in the basement, he discovered that the room was camouflaged by a virtually indetectable slant of the ceiling beams.

Emerging the next day only because he was hungry, he had convinced his mother and the disbelieving Janey that he had merely sneaked past them and out of the house. After that he vanished into his place for lengthy periods, several days at a time, bringing food with him, tracing the agitated activities of his mother and Janey by the creaking floorboards, hearing his mother's sorrow and worry over him, Janey's frustration and fury.

He had continued to come to his place periodically, through the basement window if his mother was away, entering the house the conventional way if she was home. The house never changed. The warm dark peace of his place was invaded only by the muted dramatics of his mother and Janey's television programs. And by his awareness that his mother and Janey were much more than friends.

He could not confront them with what he had discovered without drawing attention to the reason for his knowledge. But he made up for it by sneering at queers in front of them. He knew full well that his mother had demanded, on pain of separation, silence from the rebellious Janey, and he loved seeing Janey's face purple with helpless rage at his taunts.

"Mrs. Clark," the woman cop said, "you saw the knife. Does it belong to your son?"

His mother's wailing sob scraped across his nerves. A voice offered gruffly, " 'Tis his." Janey's voice.

The dyke bitch was actually turning him over to the cops! Raging, his fists clenched, he stared into the darkness. If only the cops knew the bitch was queer, had turned his mother queer . . .

A male cop said in a quiet, gentle voice, "He's been a real trial to you, hasn't he?"

"More than any mother should ever have to bear," Janey said.

"A nightmare," sobbed his mother. "The shame he's brought. Every day I pray to God for salvation for this evil child of mine who brings only hurt to others."

His mind convulsed with fury, then immediately released as he decided on his revenge. He would do what he'd done when that bitch Janey had talked his mother into throwing him out of the house. Come in the basement window with sacks of spiders, mice, ants, beetles, cockroaches, anything he could find. This time he'd even bring in rats. Then he could listen to the shrieks as that bitch and his mother found the creepy crawlies in their bed and clothing and devouring their food. Chuckling, he picked up his bottle of bourbon, and set it down moments later with a satisfied *thunk*.

"What was that," said one of the cops.

He grinned.

"Probably a mouse," said his mother. "I declare they nest in the foundations, but the exterminator people never find anything. I don't know where all the insects come from. I smell things. I hear . . . sounds from time to time."

Just me, Ma. He was hiding his face in his T-shirt sleeve, chortling with glee.

"Frank was over this morning helping us get the plants and such taken care of, you see," Janey said. "We planned to stay at his house a day or two — "

Why? What was this about? he wondered, shifting in his place, taking another pull on his bourbon. His cousin Frank lived — had lived — only a mile or so away.

" — And Janey and I were out getting a few groceries to bring along with us. If we'd only been here — " His mother broke off into sobs.

"Yes, ma'am," the male cop said kindly. "Why don't you two just relax now while we finish up here?"

Voices rose and fell throughout the morning and early afternoon. There seemed to be a lot of activity in the house considering he'd put the knife into Frank outside in the yard . . . He dozed, listening to the floor creak continually with footsteps, voices murmuring in conversation. He imagined fleets of photographers, technicians looking for fingerprints, cops writing reports and searching for evidence — all because of him.

The odor of coffee reached him. His mother serving coffee to *cops*. He lay in his place sipping bourbon resentfully, and soon unwrapped a salami sandwich, devouring all but the crusts which he hurled into a corner. I'll get her for this, he thought. I'll get them both.

"We're almost finished here," said the woman cop. "It's just as well you're leaving too. For your own peace of mind, till your neighbors all settle down. If we need anything more we'll be back tomorrow. Are you *certain* there's nowhere close by your son could be hiding? We've blanketed the area, had helicopter reconnaissance — no sign of him, nobody in the area's even seen him."

"Those government people, after he deserted, they swore he was in here, they looked in the furnace, the ducts, everywhere."

"Well, we're satisfied with our search in here."

His mother began to cry again; there were Janey's comforting tones. Then feet marched over the floorboards and out of the house.

Chuckling triumphantly, he lay back. Then he looked around the dimness of his place with a crafty grin. Lots of creepy crawlies were right in here with him. He'd just catch as many as he could in his food sack, transfer them to the upper reaches of the house to await his mother's return. He'd bring in more lots more later, when the coast was clear. Deftly, he bagged a spider.

Outside the old house, on the veranda, Officer MacKinnon closed her notebook. She and Officer Powell and Jane O'Grady watched two men in dark brown uniforms seal and padlock the door, post a huge warning sign.

One of the dark-uniformed men, the name JIM on his breast pocket, said solemnly, "It's all sealed up tight as a drum, Miss O'Grady, every door and window. I flatout *guarantee* this'll kill every single vermin in your house."

Jane O'Grady nodded, then walked toward the Volkswagen Beetle where her lover sat, head in her hands. "I'd put up with insects forever," Jane muttered, "if they could somehow exterminate just one vermin . . . "

Behind her a dark plastic shroud fluttered around the house in the gentle spring wind. The red lettered sign warned:

DANGER
POISON! FUMIGATION!
ALL PERSONS ARE WARNED TO KEEP AWAY
PREMISES ARE BEING FUMIGATED
WITH POISON GAS

XESSEX

Templeton asked hesitantly, after a glance at the unpronounceable five-word name on the manifest, "What may we call you?" In the dim light of the Station control room he smoothed a self-conscious, scarred hand over his forest green uniform jacket.

"You may call me Raj." The voice was light, musical, the words formed with awkwardness.

The Phaetan had come aboard Aries Station with proper credentials so far as Templeton could see; but he could concentrate on verification scan for only a few seconds at a time. Farlan, assigned to check the computer spec sheets, also stood transfixed and staring, boots seeming rooted to the stalamac floor.

"Raj," repeated Templeton.

"Yes, Commander," said Raj, supernaturally blue eyes drifting over to fix burningly on Farlan. "Monitor from Phaeta, by order of Godden, for one rote." The words were uttered as if memorized.

Released from the Phaetan's gaze, Templeton said with more assurance, "Everything has passed scan."

"Yes. And what are you called?" Raj inquired of Templeton's partner.

"N . . . Neal Farlan." Farlan cleared his throat and clasped his hands behind him, shiny black boots scuffing harshly on the metallic floor. "Neal Farlan, ma'am."

"Ma'am? What is ma'am? I was not taught such a word. My name is Raj."

The Phaetan was distinctly female in appearance, and surpassingly beautiful, the most beautiful creature Templeton had ever seen. Clad in a simple gold-edged scarlet tunic — perhaps a ceremonial costume as were their own green Space Service jackets — Raj was slender, statuesque, exquisitely curved. Cobalt blue eyes were fringed with thick blond eyelashes; shoulder length spun gold hair framed high cheekbones, a thin straight nose, and lips as tenderly shaped as the tiny ferns Templeton grew in the humid greenhouse of Aries Station.

"Excuse — I didn't mean to offend — " Farlan, mottled red with embarrassment, stammered further apology, wide dark eyes fastened on the golden apparition.

Templeton, realizing that Raj had not asked his name, looked on with a grin. Then he stared incredulously as the Phaetan's silken skin flushed from its pale ivory color into glowing peach. He found his voice as Farlan, also gaping, faltered into silence. "We've heard little of your planet, other than it recently sealed agreement with ExxTel as a primary source of biurnium ore."

"Yes," said Raj, and continued in a pleasing lilt, "We do not travel much, or for long. Our lovely planet is dark. We do not react well to light. In light we are . . . as you, when you are in water. That problem can be easily solved, of course. But being off our world for longer than a rote or two at very most seems to cause within us — " Raj paused and gestured gracefully. " — psychic damage."

"I see," Templeton said, and grinned again in the twilight dimness of Aries station. "Do many others on your world . . . look like you?"

Raj considered him for a moment and then responded as if to an utterly preposterous question, "Of course." With an ineffably sweet smile at Farlan, Raj extended a slender hand with long tapering fingers tipped with silver fingernails. "Nealfarlan, would you bring me to my . . . quarters?"

"Of . . . of course." Farlan took the delicate hand as if he had been given an egg shell to hold. "Neal, call me Neal."

The Phaetan turned roseate pink, and gazed at Farlan with rapidly blinking gold eyelashes. Templeton thought, If Raj isn't flirting I never saw flirting before in my life. Good luck, he thought with amusement. You'll need it with a Trad like Farlan.

Farlan asked in a voice that crackled with anxiety, "Sir, may I have your permission to escort our guest?"

"Have I . . . gone against custom?" Raj asked, blue gaze enveloping both men.

As Commander of Aries Station, it was Templeton's prerogative to accord the hospitality of ExxTel to its guests — the few there ever were. He said, "Not at all, Raj. Customs here are no matter. I'll finish up the specs," he added to Farlan, and dropped one eyelid in a half-wink.

Farlan scowled in response and turned away, to Raj.

Closed-minded young fool, Templeton thought for an innumerable time, and watched them, Farlan tall and lean and broad-shouldered, dark hair fluttering around the collar of his green jacket as he strode down the corridor; and Raj, slender and golden, an arm through Farlan's, swaying with the grace of a willow on Earth, the Earth Templeton had put out of his mind.

He finished up the specs, concentrating on his task, and limped over to the monitors. From the status readouts he could see that the *Comstock* was almost loaded, a matter of a dozen or so hours before it would automatically disengage and journey to Moon Station. It would take approximately one rote — equivalent to not quite seven Earth days — to unload the twenty ExxTel transport ships from Phaeta, including the command ship which had carried Raj, and reload the biurnium on the *Kimberly*.

Odd, he thought. Odd that such a responsible command should be entrusted to so delicate a creature. But then he knew very well that there were many permutations in the galaxy. Perhaps the "male" equivalent on Raj's planet was similar to the ethereal intellectual elite on Nexus-five, totally lacking in corporeal substance except for the means and will to procreate through selected brood partners. Perhaps that was the reason for Raj's immediate and unmistakable interest in the youthful, virile Farlan.

Flashing red light from a screen caught his eye. He had evaluated the problem before the soft hooting of the trouble siren echoed in the control room. Shifting cargo had knocked one of the unloading robots into such a position that it could not right itself. He tapped instructor keys with certainty, and an extractor claw deftly removed offending bars of spilled biurnium so that an android could right the robot and reset its controls. The red light vanished; the siren cut off.

He took little satisfaction in his accomplishment, reflecting placidly that the simplest computer could have activated the same assembly line repair. Indeed, a simple computer would have prevented the only major production "accident" that had ever occurred on Aries Station. From ExxTel's point of view, the accident that befell Templeton could *only* have happened to a man. True, a basic defect in the Station's construction had allowed seepage of fantacid, but a robot or android would have completed the repairs in a fraction of the time; no damage would have been done like the infection in his face and leg.

"Symbiotic organism," the doctors had said of his fantacid-infected body when he had finally been treated. "Harmless, unless we disturb it."

And so Aries Station had become his home. He had reasoned that if he took ExxTel to court and won all the money on Earth, what good would it be to him? As the ancient nursery rhyme so aptly said, All the king's horses and all the king's men couldn't put Gray Templeton back together again. And in exchange for waiver of his legal rights, ExxTel was willing to leave him here, provided he passed the biannual psych tests.

Here he was insulated from the emotional blows he would have suffered on Earth from his disfigurement; he was comfortable, sufficiently amused by the entertainment modes, well-taken care of. Other wants and needs he had put firmly out of his mind.

He knew he performed a function of some value, although he was cynically aware that men and women were no longer really needed in space. Alien contact and the resulting severe convulsions had ensured that. With interplanetary travel almost entirely trade, and accomplished by robot ship with communication and data transmitted by computer, a Station Commander's prime function was fulfilled when aberrant worlds occasionally declared themselves enemy and launched attack; then the Commanders transmitted early warning information until they were flamed into oblivion.

ExxTel did not publicize the fact that Aries Station had had to be rebuilt nine times in the two century interval before Templeton's arrival. But ExxTel lavishly praised its Space Service:

YOU ARE ELITE, YOU ARE HEROES, YOU WHO
WEAR THE FOREST GREEN OF EARTH AND WORK
IN THE VASTNESS OF SPACE . . .

Templeton smiled ruefully. He was a brightly plumaged
security guard who watched over a glorified warehouse. He
would some day probably die out here, his name his only
legacy, etched somewhere on a list of forgotten heroes.

He took some satisfaction from overseeing the bright
young people assigned here for various reasons by ExxTel.
Bright, promising young people. Except for Farlan. Templeton
winced, thinking about Farlan and the Trads.

Other world civilizations had reverted to their own
versions of dark ages upon alien contact, reviving ancient rites
and customs in fierce determination to maintain their identity
and the moral history of their worlds; and so also on Earth
such a sect had formed. The Traditionalists. Patterned in
behavior and belief after an era Templeton considered
barbaric: pre-twentieth century.

Farlan had been recruited into the Service in spite of his
fanatical beliefs, because of his mathematical genius. But
Templeton was convinced that the intolerant Trads were
misfits anywhere in the Space Service, whatever their gifts.
Midway in his three month tour of duty, Farlan was a
stalamac-headed bore and a constant irritant as far as
Templeton was concerned; but he intended to be fair. He had
seen no reason thus far to turn in anything but a favorable
report.

Templeton returned his thoughts to a more pleasurable
concern, the Phaetan visitor. As usual, ExxTel had supplied a
paucity of information. The laconic message from
headquarters at Pacifica had read:

PHAETAN EMISSARY. APPROVAL GODDEN. ETA
0250301. EARTH TYPE. USUAL COURTESIES.

Earth-type indeed, snorted Templeton, and punched in a computer query. Impatiently but thoroughly, he read the voluminous chemical and mineral data blipping down the screen, and extracted the facts that Phaeta was Earth-size, heavily clouded, with ivory vegetation, high H_2O content and almost constant misty precipitation, no ocean covering equivalent to Earth's but multitudinous large bodies of water. The high land mass was heavy in biurnium element, ranging from six to ten percent.

CULTURAL DATA read the next heading. Lines of print flowed down the screen.

MATURATION LEVEL NINE
LIFE EXPECTANCY LEVEL EIGHT
TECHNOLOGY LEVEL TEN PLUS RESTRICTED
POPULATION LEVEL STABLE FIVE
NON-MONOGAMOUS HUMANOID TO FACTOR
NINETY-FOUR POINT TWO

"Hmpf," said Templeton, rubbing his damaged face.

VEGETARIAN
TELESTHESIA DEVELOPMENT LEVEL THREE

Now *that* is *damn* interesting, thought Templeton. Raj read feelings — not thought — and from a distance. Interesting.

THEOLOGY LEVEL ONE

"Pantheists," Templeton interpreted, nodding approval.

POLITICAL ACTIVITY LEV —

He cancelled the program. "Seems like a nice little planet so far," he said aloud, grinning at the screen. "Why ruin my illusions?"

At dinner Templeton made laborious conversation. Raj, bare-shouldered in a clinging pale green garment, had brought food, of course, and ate an assortment of ivory-colored leaves and bean-shaped vegetables with two curved implements reminiscent of ancient Chinese chopsticks, wielding them with dexterous grace. Farlan was monosyllabic, scraping his fork unseeingly over the contents of his plate as he stared at Raj; his face was pale and drawn with tension, mottling with red when the caressing blue gaze flowed over him. Raj's silken skin blended through shades of amber. Templeton picked his way carefully through simple subjects, mostly the topical features of Phaeta.

Farlan blurted unexpectedly, "Do you have a husband?"

Raj's gold eyelashes blinked in bewilderment.

"Mate. Uh, partner." Farlan groped for other synonyms as Raj gazed. "Does someone . . . stay with you, live with you?"

"Ah." Raj brightened to a cherry pink. "No. But we do not live as you live . . . together. It is different."

"Yes. I expect it is. It doesn't matter anyway." Farlan rose and said unhappily, "Please excuse me. I have . . . duties. Forgive me." He walked stiffly from the room, squaring his broad shoulders. Templeton looked at him with a mixture of pity and disgust.

"I do not understand," Raj said, reverting to pale ivory, which seemed to be the Phaetan's normal quiescent color.

"I don't wonder. Yes," he added, seeing that Raj would not comprehend his colloquialism.

"Neal desires me. I am able to know that is true."

"Yes," Templeton, remembering the Phaetan's telesthetic capacity.

"Why does Neal not permit me to grant desire?"

He said, astounded, "You're willing to?"

"I know of your body structure. It was part of my briefing. I am able to."

"With an *Earthman?* You're *willing* to?"

"Neal has desire."

"It doesn't always work quite that way on our world. Desire doesn't always lead to . . . "

Tinkling silvery laughter expressed Raj's derision for this peculiar behavior. "This is part of your . . . courtship pattern?"

"Not always." Templeton leaned his head to one side, thrust his good leg forward at a cocky angle, and grinned. "I'm willing. I have desire for you too, even if I'm ugly."

"Not ugly." With an elegant gesture at Templeton's disfigured face and leg, Raj said, "Hurt, not ugly. But you do not have the desire like Neal. It is . . . interest only. You are content as you are."

Silenced, Templeton contemplated Raj, tucking his leg back under him. My face and leg aren't the only dead parts of me, he thought.

The cobalt eyes, objective, held his. He realized that Raj had not altered in color since Farlan had left.

"The changing tones of your skin," he said to deflect Raj's disturbing attention. "Is that part of *your* courtship pattern?"

"What we feel is spoken truly with the colors of our bodies," Raj said simply. "We have no need for some of your words."

"I see." Templeton felt oddly chastened.

"Explain to me please about Neal."

"I'll try." He searched for simple words, concepts. "It's our culture, but a step backward into our past culture. A sect on my world called Traditionalists. They demand that all people have one way of living, one way of belief, one mate, one God which judges and condemns."

"Do you think — " Raj paused. "Do you think Neal . . . will become well?"

As Templeton roared with laughter, the Phaetan appeared taken aback. "Perhaps," he said. "I don't know. He's young."

Raj rose, willow-graceful. "I will go to Neal."

"Good luck."

Raj turned back inquiringly.

"A wish that good things will happen," Templeton said.

Raj smiled.

Before he turned in, Templeton went as usual into the greenhouse. Through the leafy ferns and plants he saw Farlan with Raj's slender body clasped in his arms, his dark eyes sulphurous with desire. Raj's arms were wound around his shoulders, fingers stroking his neck, his hair. Raj's body pulsated waves of deepening rose.

Raj murmured indecipherably. "Yes," said Farlan in a husky rasp.

Templeton ducked behind a row of ferns as they left, an arm around each other, Farlan's hand caressing down over the voluptuous curve of hip. Templeton grinned, and limped over to inspect his newest ferns. That damn alien is right, he conceded. I've finally managed not to need a thing. Not a damn thing.

The next day Farlan did not appear. There was a note in the control room:

Have advised Pacifica am returning on the Comstock.
Farlan

The freighter had already departed; Templeton switched on the communicator, dialed the *Comstock's* frequency. The figure on the screen was in space gear; there was no reason for ExxTel to provide oxygen atmosphere in its robot-manned freighters.

"I have nothing to say," Farlan said with cold finality.

Templeton demanded, "I have a right to know what happened between you and Raj, whether that creature is dangerous."

Farlan did not respond, his dark imperviglas headgear motionless.

"You've ruined your career." Templeton's voice was harsh, factual.

"I don't care. I've decided Trads don't belong in the Space Service anyway."

Templeton thought, I hope you make ExxTel realize that. But he argued with the unresponsive Farlan, feeling it was his duty, until the *Comstock* was outside recall frequency. He could not have recalled the *Comstock* anyway for other than a Phase IV emergency, and the return of a misguided young genius could hardly qualify. But it would look better for the young man's future if his report could state that Farlan had changed his mind or at least regretted his act.

He signed off and sought Raj in the command cabin of the transport vessels. The Phaetan, clad in a tunic of ice blue, sat in motionless austere beauty, gazing into the star-specked blackness.

Templeton dropped heavily into a seating module. "What happened?"

"I do not know," Raj said sadly.

Templeton smothered a snort of impatience. "I saw you in the greenhouse, how the two of you were. What happened?"

"In my quarters there was a merging of our naked bodies," Raj said in a musical voice. "The rapture of Neal took me to the furthest spectrum of color."

"I see," Templeton said, disconcerted. He cleared his throat. "Then what happened?"

"I said to Neal that such complete fusion between bodies was rare on my world and resulted in the begetting of young."

"Aaahhh," breathed Templeton, his gaze sweeping in alarm over the elegant female form before him.

"Neal said the same. Neal was — " Raj's hands made motions of agitation.

"Upset. Disturbed," supplied Templeton. "I can well imagine."

"Truly. He asked then would I be procreating." Raj trilled with laughter.

"But you said — "

"It is the other members of my species which are in appearance like you who procreate."

Templeton leaped to his feet. "You mean you're a *man*?"

Raj's forehead knitted faintly. "Yes, I am by your definition male. Neal also asked that question and was — " Raj's hands again made agitated motions.

Templeton sat down again.

Raj said, "Male. Female. This is important . . . in your culture?"

"To a Trad. Don't concern yourself."

"I have been . . . in sorrow."

"Don't be, anymore. I'm sure . . . I'm sure — " Templeton stumbled over his words. "Well, you're a very special — you're kind."

"You are also . . . kind."

The cobalt blue eyes on his seemed molten. Templeton asked haltingly, "Do you think . . . that's all I can ever be?"

"No," Raj said, and turned from him to again contemplate the starry universe.

He went back to his quarters, and sat on his bed. And laughed for a while because he didn't know what else to do. Then he lay back, hands behind his head, and reflected, and imagined, releasing the aspect of his being he had frozen away for many years. His thoughts became more and more vivid.

He sat up and dialed the command vessel. "Would you have dinner with me, Raj?"

"Of course." Raj added softly, "I believe I can also arrange to come to Aries Station for a rote or two from time to time."

Templeton looked more closely at his vidiscreen and with a rush of joy saw that Raj was a warm shade of blushing pink.

FORCE MAJEUR

Joan Bronson Randall's father was dying.

Summoned from the family mill in mid-afternoon, she had been at the hospital only a few minutes when the dour young heart specialist gave her the prognosis.

"He knows, Mrs. Randall," Doctor Lynn told her. "All he wants now is to see you."

Sitting beside his bed amid the humming machinery of the intensive care unit, she rubbed cold hands over the rough corduroy and heavy cotton of her work clothes, shaking her head in stubborn denial at the sight of her father clad in white and hooked up to gauges and hanging bottles of fluid. She looked at the stocky body she had always thought so indestructible, at the strong spiky hair the color of a battleship,

67

then into Daniel Bronson's eyes. Her own slender body and dark hair were her mother's, but these were her eyes; she had inherited the exact vital blue color that was now, incredibly, fading.

"Tell me again," her father said, "about Harry. Tell me again . . . now. That you love him. That you're happy. Then I'll die believing it."

"I *hate* him." It was the first time she had spoken her profound emotion, and the rush of relief made her tremulous.

Her father stared at her.

She swallowed. "I thought I was too smart to be taken in — I was twenty-six, after all. I should have listened to you."

She couldn't tell her father, even now, that she had hurled herself at the seemingly innocuous Harry Randall. That it was Paula Gilliam who had panicked her into taking on the protective coloration of marriage. Paula, who had suffered enough trauma in her thirty-seven years as a lesbian to be defiant about their affair, and had threatened highly public exposure if Joan tried to end the relationship. By the time Joan had decided that far worse fates existed than disclosure of her sexual identity, she had been trapped in such a fate: her marriage to Harry Randall. So ensnared that she dared not even explore the deepening feeling between herself and Wilma Burke.

She said to her father, "He was . . . a terrible mistake. He was . . . in the right place at the wrong time."

"I knew he was after your money." Her father's voice was weak but scornful. "Saw right through him."

"It didn't take me all that long either," she said bitterly. "But Mother was much too sick for me to do anything. I didn't want to inflict any more suffering . . . " She trailed off, dreading the direction of this conversation.

His gaze sharpened, bored into her. "Martha's been gone eight months now. Why haven't you done anything to get rid of that scum?"

She swallowed again, then plunged ahead. "Dad, he saw you ... with Mother ... "

She was struck dumb as her father's face sagged in shock, as his eyes widened in horrified comprehension.

"Now I understand," her father whispered. "About everything." He squeezed his eyes shut.

Agonized by the pain distorting his face, she took his hand, careful of the tubes and clamps. She longed to retract her impulsive decision to justify to this beloved, dying man the deceit of the past year and a half.

"He said they'd arrest you. Exhume Mother's body. All the publicity . . . you'd go to jail . . . Dad, I couldn't let it happen—" The hand in hers gripped firmly, silencing her.

At last her father said, "I loved your mother so very much. Your mother asked ... What I did was — "

"Dad," she interrupted, "don't explain. I know how much she was suffering. She was your wife but she was my mother."

"Joanie," he said brokenly.

She rose, kissed his wet face.

Some time later he said, "Get rid of Harry now." Anger had strengthened his voice. "I'd give anything to do it myself. Where is he?"

"Camping as usual," she said tersely.

"I've heard he shares his camper with feminine company." His face was drawn, grayish, but he looked at her shrewdly.

Her smile was sour. "I know all about her. Not that I care."

"Give him money, that's what he wants. Get him away from you." His voice had risen again. "Promise me. Whatever you need to do." His hand gripped hers.

"Dad, you have to rest," she said, alarmed by the darkening gray of his color.

"Whatever you need to do," he said tiredly, closing his eyes. "Promise me."

"I promise."

Her father's grip loosened; he was asleep, breathing raggedly.

Outside the intensive care unit she asked Doctor Lynn, "How long?"

He cleared his throat. "Hard to tell, Mrs. Randall. But his blood pressure's dropping fast."

"How can it be so hopeless?" she demanded. "How could this happen?"

Doctor Lynn ran a hand through his unruly brown hair and said with a trace of anger, "How could your father ignore classic heart attack symptoms till it was much too late to help him?"

Joan lowered her gaze, thinking of her father's unremitting grief for her mother.

An hour later she sat beside her father's bed holding his hand again. He momentarily opened his dim eyes to whisper, "You're Joan Bronson again." Later he said in a firm voice, "It's Wilma you need beside you."

She gaped at him. Wilma Burke was the company comptroller — an important but not vital position. What did he mean?

Not even her mother possessed the uncanny insight into her that her father did . . . He might very well have discerned her carefully guarded feeling for Wilma, that her attraction to this big gentle woman had strengthened well beyond admiration. Though she had kept Wilma at arm's length, having too little of herself to offer her, she knew that beneath Wilma's quiet, undemanding loyalty was an answering attraction. Could he have somehow guessed?

His eyes might have revealed an answer. But they remained closed.

I do love her . . .

As her father shook his head and sighed deeply she wondered frantically, Did I think that — or did I actually say it?

He did not open his eyes as he said, "I love you, Joanie."

She squeezed her eyes shut to keep back the tears but she could not keep them from her voice: "I love you, Dad."

He was silent for a long time. When he spoke again he was delirious. Joan realized that his words were endearments to her mother.

· In Longview, Washington, at five minutes to six that evening, Saturday, May 17, 1980, Daniel Bronson died.

She did the few things left to be done for her father: preliminary arrangements with Chapman's, the same funeral home which had buried her mother; the brief but necessary phone calls to Uncle David and Aunt Lucy, to Gerald and Agnes and Donald, the relatives and friends dearest to her father, who received her news with disbelief, then inarticulate grief. She did not call Wilma Burke. She knew very well that the sound of those warm, caring tones would dissolve the fine-edged, fragile control that was allowing her to act.

One last item remained. Now that her father's body lay in a funeral home, she would not allow Harry Randall to enjoy the Bronson money for one hour longer. She would not wait for Harry Randall to wander home.

Shortly before midnight, she turned off Highway 5 onto the curves and darkness of Highway 504. The smell of pine was sharp, the icy night air engulfed her from the open window, welcome on her flushed face. Driving the Jeep swiftly past the large, orange-lettered signs warning campers away, she remembered how her father had taught her to drive on the roads into the lumber yards and rough logging country of Bronson Paper Products. She always had preferred the Jeep's honest simplicity to the soft comforts of her other cars. Beside her on the seat were wadded up tissues discarded as she drove. She cried ceaselessly, shaken by grief and bitterness and anger.

She whetted and fanned her anger with vivid memories of Harry's face — a weak face mirroring the true character of a man she had once believed she could trust, a face she had even fleetingly thought poetically handsome. The face that had distorted into an ugly mask of gloating as he made his blackmail demands. Then there had been the slow torture of his increasing extortions. The town gossip over his flagrant infidelities with his former girlfriend Bonnie Davis, who looked at Joan with bold, contemptuous eyes. The camper Joan had been forced to buy — but at least that had been a good investment; for the past three months Harry had been gone much of the time with Bonnie Davis.

She had had no choice but to stand loyally with her father. Every other option in her life was closed off. She could only live from day to day and work hard and prepare herself for the time she had assumed would be far distant — when she inherited Bronson Paper Products.

The bright yellow camper was parked on a bluff overlooking Spirit Lake; the headlights of the Jeep picked it out easily.

Harry finally answered her insistent pounding.

"What the hell're you doing here?" Bleary-eyed, with a heavy stubble of beard, he stood in the camper's doorway, his arms crossed over monogrammed blue silk pajamas. The camper exuded the sweet brackish smell of marijuana.

"My father's dead," she said evenly, staring at him with unblinking contempt.

He stared back at her. "You're not kidding, are you. You look terrible. When?"

Her tone was vitriolic. "This evening. A massive heart attack."

Scratching his beard, he contemplated her.

Loathing this man who had degenerated beyond the simple decency of speaking a word of condolence, Joan said, "Go back and pack up your things and get out. Take whatever you want. I want every trace of you gone."

"Not so fast." Bonnie Davis pulled a fleecy red robe around her as she came to the door. She pushed disheveled dark hair out of her eyes. "Not so fast, sister." She turned to Harry. "I thought you were smart. Don't you see what's happened? This is beautiful! You're married to an heiress, to all that money!"

"I had that figured out already," Harry said, but his dark eyes were stunned. "The jackpot, we've hit the jackpot!"

Joan cursed herself for her shortsightedness. "You . . . leech!" She spat the word at him.

"You'll pay for that." His voice was low and cold. "Try and guess what the leech's gonna do now." He turned to Bonnie Davis. "Just listen to how smart I can be." He jerked a thumb at Joan. His grin was slow, malevolent. "She gives us what we want or we swear she told us all about her father bumping off her mother. That makes her accessory to murder — "

"You can't do this," Joan uttered.

"No? Just watch." Harry's voice rose. "And I'm gonna love every sweet minute. How do you think I felt when you and your snob father looked at me like I was nothing, like I belonged in a garbage dump!"

"You'll show 'em now, honey." Bonnie Davis linked her arm possessively, triumphantly through Harry's.

He was glaring at Joan as he said, "We'll both show 'em, baby. How'd you like to run Bronson Paper Products with me?"

Frozen with the vision of this new nightmare, Joan whispered, "You can't do this."

"Just watch me." His narrowed eyes drifted over her heavy wool shirt, her corduroy pants. "So, Joanie-phony, climb in your big dyke Jeep and beat it."

"Yeah," Bonnie smirked. "Get lost, dyke."

Harry slammed the door. Faintly, Joan heard laughter.

Her father had said: *Whatever you need to do.*

She unlocked the glove compartment of the Jeep and took out the .32, fitting the cold, foreign shape into her fingers. She stared at the gray metal object, trying to summon up reserves of determination.

Then, struck by an idea, she put the gun down on the seat and sat perfectly still, appraising the position of the camper on the bluff.

Suddenly she started the engine, gunning it hastily as if the camper would move of its own volition if she did not act quickly on her impulse.

She aligned the front of the Jeep with the rear of the camper. The thought occurred that the camper's emergency brake would be on. She floored the Jeep's accelerator. The camper lurched forward and stopped.

Desperately, she gunned the powerful engine. The camper skidded slowly forward across the soft dirt of the bluff.

The camper door was flung open and Bonnie's broad, astonished face gaped at her. The camper inched ever so slowly ahead.

"What the hell you doing!" Bonnie screamed. "Harry!"

Joan picked up the gun, waved it out the window. To her amazement, splinters flew from the wood frame of the camper doorway: she had pulled the trigger. Bonnie stared for a single unbelieving instant, then slammed the door.

Joan looked at the gun; it slipped from her fingers into her lap. She pushed it off frenziedly, as if it were a snake. What *was* she doing? How could she conceivably act as executioner of two human lives? She threw the Jeep into reverse gear, clouds of dust rising as the wheels spun in the soft dirt.

The camper door was jerked open. Harry peered out at her. In a surge of revulsion she seized the gun; he dodged backward. She hurled the weapon far out into the water.

"Bitch, you're dead!" he screamed, leaning out the camper door. "Tomorrow your ass is in jail, tomorrow you're gonna..."

She roared off in the Jeep, cutting off further invective.

On her way back to Longview she calculated that perhaps a dozen more hours of freedom were left to her. Harry would roll out of bed late as usual, then come down the mountain and have her arrested for attempted murder. His evidence would be incontestible: the bullet hole, the tire track marks on the bluff, scratches and paint chips on the front of her Jeep. She had thrown a gun registered to her into the water; the weapon could be found. Even though activity in the area where Harry liked to camp had sharply decreased after all the warnings, some of the few remaining campers and hikers had probably heard the gunshot. And the motive for attempted murder would be obvious. She smiled wryly. Joan Bronson's mind had snapped after the death of her father, and the long-suffering, jealous wife had come after her philandering husband and the other woman.

Dispirited, grieving, exhausted, she parked the Jeep and went into her house and sank onto the sofa and dissolved into tears.

Asleep in her clothes on the sofa, she was jarred awake by the telephone. It was shortly after eight-thirty in the morning. She was unprepared for the gentle, reproachful voice of Wilma Burke.

"Joan, I just heard. I can't believe Daniel's dead. I can't believe you didn't call me last night."

"Wilma, I... I needed time."

"I can understand that. But..." She sighed. "Joan, I... I always felt you'd call me if you needed... help."

"I do need help, Wilma. I need you more than you know," Joan said shakily. "More than you want," she added.

"Not possible," Wilma said softly. "Joan, I'll be here."

Unable to speak further, sickened by the vision of the night before, Joan hung up. Harry would be coming down the mountain soon now, and then the police would be here . . .

Her eyes were drawn and then riveted to an expanding, exploding cloud of darkness outside her living room window. The horizon was slowly vanishing in an enveloping mass of boiling blackness.

Hair pricked along the nape of her neck. She thought numbly, Is this it, an atomic attack? Or —

She ran to the radio, searched for a news broadcast.

". . . about eight-thirty this morning. A scientific team is believed encamped on the slopes, their fate is unknown at this time. Nor is the fate of others in the vicinity, including famed eighty-four year old recluse Harry Truman who refused to be evacuated from his home near Spirit Lake. The cloud of volcanic dust and debris from Mount St. Helens has spread many miles into the atmosphere and is moving at this very moment over the city. Longview city officials urge all citizens to remain indoors, to be calm — "

The phone shrilled. "Did you hear? Do you see what's happening?"

"Wilma," she said in a trembling voice, "Harry was there . . . right beside that mountain in a camper . . . and I — "

"After all the warnings? The fool! Why on earth _ " She broke off. "As if you haven't been through enough with Daniel. Let me take care of this, Joan, notify the authorities. Everything'll be done that can be done."

"Wilma, wait, You don't understand — "

"I do understand, trust me. You need to rest, take care of yourself. I'll be with you as soon as I can." She hung up.

Absently, her eyes fixed on the cataclysmic sky, Joan sleepwalked her way to her radio and turned it up, then switched on the television set.

Hours later, sitting on her living room sofa very close to Wilma Burke who held her hand in loving comfort, Joan was still listening to the disaster reports, still staring in bemusement at the sky as pale ash coated her grass and flowers and trees and house.

MOTHER WAS AN ALIEN

The idea to smuggle Mother off Verna III came to father when Jed Peterman fell down a hill of keteraw and proceeded to smother in a pile of mutherac, managing to do this in spite of all his training and thorough briefings on the planet's topography. Father, his crew chief, found him, and in disgust kicked him further down the hill, starting an avalanche which buried poor Peterman forever.

Why would Father risk years of severe punishment to bring an alien to Earth? Mother looked like one of the Sirens of Earth legend. Glossy dark silken hair reached to her voluptuous hips and covered cantaloupe-sized breasts. As if that wasn't enough to capture a young Earthman there were her extraordinarily beautiful eyes — the color of pure emerald.

And Mother, an inexperienced Vernan child of only forty-five, was enthralled with Father's virility and willing to go with him anywhere.

Father cut Mother's hair to collar length and concealed her remarkable eyes in gray infra-protect lenses. Judicial application of plastisculpt coarsened her nose and chin and ears. The barest touch of a surgiscope knife added temporary lines around her eyes and mouth. Still, his plan would never have worked except for the flappy tents the space crews wear which hid Mother's cantaloupes.

Exercising his authority as crew chief, Father accused "Peterman" of violating Earthcode MCLVIII — sexually harassing a female alien, a misdemeanor — and imposed a sentence of solitary confinement for the duration of the return trip to Earth. Of course, only Mother's days were solitary.

Upon arrival on Earth, poor "Peterman" vanished, AWOL from the Service. And Father took Mother to the pleasure capital of Vega where he married her. So long as she did not have to be fingerprinted or have her blood tested she could easily pass as an Earth female, albeit spectacularly endowed; and given her extreme youth it was unlikely that she would face exposure through medical discovery for many years. Perhaps by then, Father reasoned, the laws would have changed. And so Mother and Father set up housekeeping in Calivada.

Mother did have her idiosyncracies. She made noises at night — sometimes like the klaxxon warning of a fluorocarbon alert, sometimes reminiscent of nineteenth century war-whooping Indians. She was by now pregnant and since Vernan babies become conscious in the womb after the first month, the first words I heard were from Father, grumbling during one of her spectacular effusions: "Great Calvin Coolidge, can't you hold that down a little? Everyone in the neighborhood knows what we're doing."

"A Payrungasmad curse on the neighbors. Can you do that again, dear?"

Father was furious when he learned of her pregnancy. "Great James Garfield, how could you let that happen!" he bellowed. "We've been married only six weeks! You said you'd take ovavoid!"

"No I didn't, you just gave me the pills," Mother informed him coolly. "I did what all Vernan females do when their males leave it up to them. Each time before we made love I concentrated hard and thought negative thoughts." She shrugged. "Sometimes it works, sometimes it doesn't."

For a while Father screamed incoherently, then asked in a hoarse voice, "Why didn't you take the pills? Why why why?"

"Those things have never been perfected in three hundred years. Imagine what they'd do to a Vernan. At least we don't have to worry about birth control for a while, dear," she said seductively. "Isn't that good?"

Father, who was accustomed to adjusting swiftly to emergencies in space, had calmed down somewhat. But he said plaintively, "What do we do now? I'll have to find someone, pay a huge bribe. Then worry about blackmail. Maybe I can think of a way to smuggle you back to Verna-Three."

"Don't worry," Mother said. "I'll manage."

Meanwhile, reports of Mother's foibles had spread throughout the district, especially after she daily emptied tea leaves from the vacuum tubes and explained to a curious neighbor that she always sprinkled tea leaves on her floors, tannic acid being wonderful for the disposition. And when another astonished neighbor watched Mother pluck choice leafy tidbits from the front hedge and eat them for her lunch, Father realized that even in Calivada Mother was a bit too outre. So he hustled her off to an isolated but fully mechanized farmhouse near the border. She did not mind in the least; pregnant Vernan women crave solitude. She spent much of her time telescanning Earth's history and culture and learning agronomy and hydroponics, which she realized we would soon need.

Vernans do not require an interminable nine months for gestation; mother and baby work together to make things much more efficient. And so five months later, Mother gave birth. It took about an hour for us to be born, one by one.

"Great Ulysses Grant!" Father screamed, tearing at his hair. "It's a goddam litter!"

"It's all your doing," Mother retorted, more than a little miffed. "The male determines the number. That's how it is on Verna. The more sperm, the more chance for more eggs to be fertilized. And Geezerak knows you're a regular sperm factory."

"Great Woodrow Wilson, how could I know that," Father said shakily as Vesta and I were born, the last two, bringing the grand total to nine, all of us girls.

"One Y chromosome," Mother grumbled at him. "You couldn't spare even one Y chromosome."

"Never again!" hollered Father. "No ovavoid pills, no more you know what!"

"Suit yourself. You could take them yourself, you know. I'll be sore for a day or two, anyway. And lower your voice," Mother said as we all began to wail, "you're disturbing the girls."

In a voice shaking with horror Father said, "Clothes! Great Herbert Hoover, clothes for nine girls!"

"I'll manage," Mother said.

"How will you ever take care of them?"

"I'll manage," Mother said.

"Even choosing names for nine girls!"

Mother said distractedly, fastening liquiblots to each of us, "The girls and I settled all that before they were born."

"What!" Father shrieked.

Frightened by him, I began to cry. "There there, Minerva," Mother cooed, picking me up. "Dear," she said to Father, "it's a . . . strong communication. It's gone, now that they're born. I can't really explain. Anyway, males never understand how it is between mothers and babies."

"What have I wrought," Father whispered, tiptoeing away.
Little did he know.

Isis was the first of us to indicate special gifts. When she was eight, Mother discovered that she had full comprehension of a teleclass in spatial calculus. I had already chosen my specialty — history — and was able to explain to my family that mathematical genius usually manifests itself quite early. It was then that Mother warned us all to be careful, that our family could not afford the bright light of publicity. Isis, soon bored with calculus, entertained herself by plotting stock market curves.

Thanks to Mother's agronomy and hydroponics expertise, the farm had become virtually self-sufficient, and Father and Mother managed to conceal our existence for quite a while. After that, although the nine of us drew attention we had grown at very different rates and were physically dissimilar. To our chagrin, we had inherited more of Father's build than Mother's; but fortunately, we had also acquired fingerprints.

Father spent more and more time away, volunteering for missions of six months and longer duration, coming home for a few weeks of loving attention from Mother, then blasting off again. It was hard to blame him. During his time home nine squealing little girls climbed all over him, but he was frustrated in his attempts to enjoy us; he was unable to win so much as a game of gin rummy or any other game of skill by the time we were six. Hera knew more about the space ships he flew than he did by the time she was eleven. He was less and less able to participate even in dinner table discussions of any kind.

As we turned sixteen, Father had been gone for more than a year. A beribboned representative form the Service visited, gazed at us in astonishment, then broke the news that Father had been last seen pursuing a fellow crewman in a shuttle craft and had vanished near a black hole.

"He was a hero," said the representative.

Hera, by now an expert in astrophysics, said through her tears, "If he'd just known to set the coordinates for — "

Mother sobbed loudly and stamped on Hera's foot.

The representative went on to explain Mother's survivor benefits. "Rough going, supporting such a big family," he said sympathetically. "Even with generous benefits."

Mother dried her tears. "I'll manage."

The stock prognostications of Isis were now invaluable. Mother's investments financed travel and advanced educations for us all.

Once we completed our home-based education and ventured out into the world we thought it would be more difficult to hide our gifts, especially when we all performed spectacularly well scholastically, and later, professionally. But we had one overwhelming advantage: We were women. Scant significance was attached to any of our accomplishments.

It was Diana, now a geneticist, and Demeter, a meditech, who made the first great contribution to our future. They discovered through experimentation that most Vernan genes were dominant and consequently mutation-resistant.

"It's why you had girls," Diana explained to Mother. "You couldn't have had a male no matter what."

Venus, our biologist, joined in further research. Additional experiments showed that our life expectancy was thirty years longer than an Earth male's; that unlike Mother who was pure Vernan, we were more likely to bear only two or three babies at most at one time, all girls; and that they would inherit the intellectual capacity of their mothers.

Selene the poet and Olympia the philosopher made the final valuable contributions, documenting and forecasting the continuing irrationality of Earth beliefs, customs, and mores, and clearly demonstrating the need for concern — and change.

We have just completed a week-long meeting of extraordinary scope, and have made our plans.

We will all marry. We will all have as many births as our individual situations allow. And pass the word on to our daughters.

Isis has shown that if we have multiple births, and succeeding generations continue at that rate, exponentially there will soon be a female population explosion.

And we are perfectly concealed. Men will continue to notice us only for their sexual and nesting needs — which is what we want them to do. And by the time they observe that there has been an astonishing number of births of baby girls, it will be much too late.

I am Minerva the historian, and this is the first chapter of our saga . . .

MANDY LARKIN

I'm in a hunting cabin near the place I was born, I'm talking into this tape recorder to explain how all this happened. Not even Mama knows to look for me here, so I can be by myself at least a while longer. It's maybe three weeks now — I've lost track of time.

Today I was all day crying over my father. It's years since I gave him even one thought, not since I was a little girl and curious about everything, especially him. Mama claimed he was just a nothing louse that ran out soon as she told him she was having me. Growing up I believed that, I put him clean out of my mind. I should of seen long before this that Mama probably hadn't an idea in the world who my father was. He might even be one of my uncles but I don't think so. Maple

Creek's a pretty small place and I've been thinking about the men there and what I know about them, because I think maybe I got the music in me from my father. I sure didn't get it from Mama.

I forgot to say who I am, I guess I'm too used to people knowing me. I'm sure it's all over the newspapers how Mandy Larkin ran off, and how nobody can figure out why I did it or where I went to.

All this happened because of the music. But I don't know how I could of stopped it because far back as I can remember, I guess from the first time I ever heard a song, I knew singing was the only thing for me to do. Up till I was eleven it was the one good thing in my life. If it hadn't filled up the days I might of ended up like Betty Lou. I heard she jumped off that barn roof because of some boy she wanted and couldn't have, but to this day I don't believe it. I think it was because she didn't have anything filling her up like I did. Betty Lou only broke some bones, but after that she never spoke another word, she just smiled and paid no heed at all to anybody till she got sent away to the looney bin. Well, come to think of it, maybe I *have* ended up like Betty Lou.

When I was nine the county people somehow found out about me and came around and told Mama and my uncles I had to go to school or there'd be trouble. Mama declared she was schooling me at home, which wasn't true, and my uncles claimed school never did any of them any good and I guess it didn't. But they let me go, they didn't care all that much except Mama complained about school letting me out of chores around the place.

But I didn't go to school hardly at all and I didn't pay much mind when I did. Back then I was just like Mama, I couldn't see past the end of my nose. Nobody I knew read books, who cared what happened to somebody in a book? That's how stupid I was in those days.

This time of year makes me think of old Miss Jenkins, the teacher. It was around Christmas when I was eleven, and she asked did we want to sing a few songs and what were the ones we liked best? So we sang Jingle Bells and Frosty the Snowman and silly things like that, and then I said, bold as you please, I really like O Holy Night. Miss Jenkins said it was pretty but too hard to sing. So I sang it to her. Miss Jenkins sat still as a cat and I'll never forget the look on her face when I got to O night divine and those real high notes. And I knew how everybody else in that class liked it too, I could feel it way deep inside me. After that a boy named Whitey asked if I'd sing anything else I liked. So I sang Shenandoah. And that sweet Miss Jenkins, soon as I sang Far away you rollin river, she had tears running down her face and it warmed me like I'd never felt before. Mama and my uncles never did pay any mind to my singing, they'd heard me every day from the time I was small.

Whitey — we called him that for his hair — he brought in a guitar the next day and made me take it even though it used to belong to his father, he died of drinking bad whiskey so they say. The guitar was old but it had all the strings, so I took it home and buffed and polished it up. After that I could make all my own music, put guitar notes with my singing.

I was thinking today maybe Whitey's father could be my father too. I cried for a long while thinking I didn't know his name or one thing about what he was like, this man who maybe had music in him like I do in me, and I see I've got to turn off this tape recorder because I'm crying again.

So anyway. I went to school more because I could sing there and Miss Jenkins found plenty of reasons to have me do it. Some way I knew just how to sing for everybody so they liked me. It was right around then that Whitey and me went

into the woods behind the school and I let him do what he
wanted, he had this good feeling about me instead of like my
uncles who did it only because they wanted to. But I didn't feel
anything special with Whitey any more than I did with my
uncles. Feeling special came awhile later, with Jaimie.

It was the Johnson wedding that changed my life for good.
I've been thinking these last weeks what I'd of become when I
grew up if it hadn't happened, and I guess I'd of ended up like
poor Mama.

To this day I can't say which Johnson girl got married, or
who it was she married. Miss Jenkins asked me to sing at the
reception and before I could say I didn't have the clothes she
said a dress from her niece would fit me just fine and Clem
Johnson would pay me twenty dollars besides — he was willing
to believe I was good just on Miss Jenkins' say so.

Singing to my classmates was one thing, but I was scared to
death about this. The Johnson place is the nicest house in
Maple Creek, and the day of the wedding I roamed around
those big pretty rooms for a long while just strumming my
guitar. But I knew I had to earn that money, so finally I sat
down in a corner and started playing and singing Shenandoah.
Everybody got quiet as mice and gathered around to listen,
even whichever Johnson girl it was got married and her new
husband.

After Shenandoah I sang lots of other songs, some of them
sprightly — after all it was a wedding — and I could *tell* what
they wanted next, how to make them happy. I just *knew* it, I
could almost *hear* it. I sang and sang till I couldn't anymore.
Then they crowded around all talking at once and smiling and
reaching out for me, and that was peculiar and a little scary.

That's when I first met Hank. I'd noticed him before, a tall
man with a little grey beard, and thick through the chest, a
fancy white shirt on him with a rope tie. He was off by himself,
touching that beard and nodding the whole time I was singing.
He pushed his way through to me and eased the guitar ever so

gently from me and took hold of my hand, he led me away and put me and my guitar in his truck.

He drove me on toward home and asked lots of questions about how my life was. Nobody'd ever done that before and there was something so warm and safe about him I answered him honest. When I told him about my uncles he pulled off the road to ask me more and more questions, and I could feel a cold angry buzz settle in him, like he was a mad bee.

When we got to my place he talked very kindly to Mama, but he was firm that she had to let me go with him where I'd have a better chance with my life, and it was the best thing she could do for me. I'd be staying with his sister who'd look after me and see I got more schooling and he'd help with my singing besides. Mama wasn't agreeing with any of this till Hank asked what kind of a life would I have in Maple Creek, and then she guessed maybe it was all right, being as how Chattanooga wasn't all that far away, and I'd be coming back a lot so she could check up on me.

But then my uncles got back from town. Uncle Duane wanted money from Hank, claiming it was plain what Hank really wanted with me.

I remember so clear the veins sticking out in Hank's neck and what he said to Uncle Duane and Uncle Sherm and how quiet he said it. You scum, he told them, you ought to be on a chain gang the rest of your unnatural lives for what you been doing to this little girl.

Uncle Duane was big as Hank, tall, a fat stomach that used to smother me when he laid himself on me. He'd slap Mama around when she sassed him, he beat up anybody that crossed him, he never stepped back from anybody. But he said to Hank in this whiny voice, Me and Sherm ain't the only ones.

Hank came after Uncle Duane then. But Uncle Sherm stepped in and pulled Uncle Duane into the house. My Uncle Sherm never did say a word to Hank, he never said much to anybody anyhow, me included.

The way Hank stood tall to my uncles like poor Mama never could do — it turned my insides every which way.

So off we went in Hank's truck to Chattanooga. I was almost fifteen by then. And that's when I first knew Hank's sister Polly. She was crippled up from a car accident that killed her husband and little boy, but she took me in like I was hers to take care of, like she didn't have any cares or sorrows at all. At Polly's I ate good food and wore nice clothes for the first time, and Polly showed me how to sew and how to keep myself neat and clean, she made me feel good about how I looked. She had a record player and I listened to country music all the time, even when I was working on a song in my head.

I went to school and that's when I found out how dumb I really was, all my classmates were so much younger. I'd paid no heed to that in Maple Creek, not with two rooms of us in the school and all of us different ages. But Polly made me go every day, and shamed as I was with all those little ones, I paid attention and worked hard and it didn't take long at all to skip over grades and almost catch up.

Hank gave me this tape recorder to carry around with me, the one I'm talking into now, so I could work on my songs and see how they sounded. He made me sing all the time, made me learn music. But I never did like to put the notes down on paper — writing songs out seemed too much like caging up a bird.

Even when I was up in the room they made for me in the attic I could tell when Hank came into the house and Polly could never figure out how I knew, she wouldn't believe how I could feel a buzz come from him whenever he was near. I could tell something about me bothered something inside him.

Hank never tried to do anything but hug me, and I asked Polly why and she said it wouldn't be right, he had his girlfriends and it was better we didn't, there was other ways we should help each other and not every man wanted to do that to every woman. Well, that was all news to me, it was plain I had a whole lot of learning and growing up to do.

I never could of gone any further than singing for kids at the high schools and such except for Hank. When I finally got my chance to sing at Lucy's Roadhouse, that first night I begged him not to make me go out on that little stage, all those strangers with their cold eyes just waiting to stare at me and not caring at all except to drink their beer. But Hank talked sweet and gentle till I finally stumbled out with my whole body like a frozen stick. Soon as I started singing I was all right and the people there loved me like crazy, but I told Hank I didn't think I could ever do it again.

Then he came up with this idea, he fixed it so next time the stage would be pitch black for me to go out onto. There I'd be with my guitar and I'd start singing Shenandoah just like I sang it to Miss Jenkins when I was eleven. So I tried it and when the spotlight came on I felt all the people loving me right away. After that I was fine, and Shenandoah was my song, the people always knew I'd sing it first.

Hank and Polly have scrapbooks about all the places I sang and how the papers said I was the sweetest voice in country music. I went to Nashville and made my first album, Mandy Larkin Sings the Songs of the Mountains, and it was so popular that one fine hot night in August I got to stand for the first time in a spotlight on the stage of the Grand Old Opry.

None of it could of happened except for Hank and Polly, and when I made my first money from singing I had the legal papers done to make them my managers so I could give something back. It was about then that Miss Jenkins wrote a nice letter telling me how proud she was. Polly helped me find a music box all fancy and pretty, and got them to make it play Shenandoah, and I sent it to Miss Jenkins. I heard she died last year, I wish I could of thanked her proper.

I gave money to Mama but I couldn't see what she did with it. More and more I couldn't stand going back to Maple Creek,

I couldn't stand how sad and tired she looked, and I plain couldn't abide my uncles. I asked Hank to go see Mama and talk to her and he told me as gentle as he could that Mama gave my uncles the money and they used it for women and drink. Hank offered to help her get away from my uncles but she wouldn't go. Now there won't be any money coming from me anymore, but I guess it won't make that much difference to Mama anyway.

After the Grand Old Opry Hank and me traveled all over doing concerts and I lived in the nicest hotels with whoever I liked at the time. I couldn't make Hank understand about that, and it was the beginning of bad times between us. Some men I met really wanted me, I could always tell, but Hank got mad as a hornet when I said they loved me because the man was always gone in a few weeks, and Hank claimed I didn't know what love really was. He was right about that but how could I know it? I hadn't met Jaimie yet, I didn't know any better.

One time Hank saw Harlan, I think that was his name, he was taking the ring Polly gave me when I turned sixteen. Hank grabbed the ring away and then he yanked Harlan right up off the floor and threw him out into the hotel hallway. Then Hank hollered at me why didn't I pick one good man and let that be the end of it. I hollered back he was the same way with his girlfriends and he yelled it wasn't the same, he was a man.

I really did try to do what he said but I could tell after a while the new man's feeling for me wasn't the same at all and I didn't want any man around doing things to me when all the good feeling was gone.

It was Birmingham where I met Jaimie, she was a backup guitar player for my show at the Fiddler Theater. She hung around my dressing room a lot, she was quiet and real shy, but I could tell she loved me — I knew it keen as knives. I'd heard about things between women but never for a second did I think it could happen to me or I'd want it if it did. But I understood pretty quick that I did, because I couldn't take my eyes off her somehow. I couldn't help but admire the free and easy way she had with herself, she seemed the freest of any woman I ever knew. I asked would she like to go on down to Mobile where I'd be singing next and she said yes right off, not even taking time to think on it.

Next to Hank she was the gentlest person, even more loving than him. No man who loved me before her understood how I was after my singing, how emptied out I was inside. She'd take me to bed and hold me and rock me like a little baby and say sweet words till I fell asleep all warm from her, and then in the morning she'd love me with even sweeter words. Her loving always seemed like it was more for me than her, she'd make me feel everything about myself, she'd love me in different ways again and again till I was emptied out in a whole other way.

At first Hank thought Jaimie and me were just friends and he was glad because we got on so well and we'd always be working on my music together, and besides there weren't any men with Jaimie around. But when I couldn't do enough for her, wanting to buy her everything I could think of even though she wouldn't take most of it, when we stayed in my hotel room late most mornings and wouldn't be apart the rest of the time, Hank pretty soon figured things out.

Even so he didn't say much except warn me to be extra careful because the people wouldn't pay to see me if they found out about Jaimie, and the newspaper reporters who thought I was the sweetest voice in country music, they'd turn on me and tear me apart. He figured too that Jaimie was like my men, she wouldn't be around all that long. But how she felt about me didn't change at all, she was all the time loving me, and living with her was just like being in the loveliest warm bath water that never gets the least bit cool.

It was five months after she was with me, the last night of my shows in Louisville, I came into my dressing room all worn out and expecting to find Jaimie, but there was only some yellow roses and a letter from her. She wrote that she didn't want to ruin me or my singing, she could see if she stayed any longer the papers and such would be bound to start noticing. She loved me and always would but she didn't see any good or right thing to do except move on.

Right away I figured her leaving to be Hank's doing. I'd seen a week or so before that Jaimie was upset, but she wouldn't say what was troubling her. Hank knew it wouldn't do one bit of good to try and talk me into leaving Jaimie, so he'd worked on her, he could see Jaimie was the kind of person who'd give herself up not to hurt me.

I went plain crazy over that letter, I was mad enough to kill. Hank claimed Jaimie'd left on her own, but when he saw how really bad I was over this, he put ads in the papers all over the South asking her to come back. I paid a detective to go out looking for her, thinking he'd find her through her music, but it seemed she'd given that up too. Somebody like Jaimie who didn't have any family to speak of because they'd kicked her out, and drifting all over the countryside as the spirit moved her, she was real hard to find. I couldn't sing at all, and Hank worried over me like never before, saying I should take some time and go off someplace. But I didn't want anything but to find Jaimie and have her with me again.

It was a month ago I decided I'd go back to singing, maybe it could help make the pain about Jaimie ease up a little. So I went off to Memphis, to the brand new Circle Club there.

I remember going into the place to rehearse, so the new lighting and stage hands could learn what they needed to do. I always liked going into the places where I was to sing. I liked to watch everybody getting things ready. There was always the same kind of smell, a theater smell, and I liked it better than any other. And every time it was as if the people were already in their seats, I could feel them sitting there. Each time I sang it seemed like I could tell deeper and deeper how they loved me, it was like whispers way deep in my head, and I could even *hear* them if I just tried hard enough.

Time and again I told Jaimie how it was about the whispering deep in my head but she'd always just smile and say it was the special feeling between me and my audience and it was why my singing was so special, I was like Judy Garland used to be in her concerts. I couldn't make Jaimie understand how I was different, that I really could hear the whispering.

You won't understand what happened to me in Memphis either, because it hasn't happened to anybody on this earth that I know of. I wouldn't have to be hiding, I wouldn't have to be telling this if it had, if anybody else was like me. I've got to tell it and hope somebody believes me.

The Circle Club was a brand new place and it felt strange to me, it had no theater smell, just paint and cloth smells from the new seats and the stage curtain. For the first time in a long while I didn't want to go out on stage. Hank talked to me gentle like he used to, but I was real stubborn and so when the house lights went down he plain pushed me out there.

Standing on that big stage all by myself in the pitch dark, I could feel the people out there. Nice and quiet like always, but I could hear their clothes, the sound clothes make when a lot of people sit together, and I could hear their breathing.

I strummed the opening chord on my guitar and just as I opened my mouth to start Shenandoah that spotlight came on and hit me. It was too early, the lighting man had got it wrong, he was supposed to wait till I got to Far away you rollin river.

I plain froze, I just *stood* there. I could make out the shadows of people in their seats, and I could *hear* all the people out there, their thoughts about me. And I couldn't *move*, I stood rooted into that stage lighted up bright as day and it was like I was naked. I'm telling you I could hear in their minds that I was skinny, that I was uglier than sin. That I was such a dumb looking hillbilly I probably didn't even shave under my arms. How the men'd like a chance to put themselves between my legs and in my mouth and turn me over and do it vicious like I was some of kind of dirty dog.

There were some thoughts about me looking nice and sweet as a child but anything warm and good got swept away in a flood of horrible mud like I can't even tell you and it all flowed right over me, over my eyes and down my throat.

I tore off that stage with my hands over my ears, and that no more stopped all the thoughts than paper stops fire.

Hank ran after me scared to death, I could hear that in his mind. And I could hear how much he loved me and he really did want to be between my legs no matter what Polly said about it, and he felt awful for wanting that because I was mixed up in his head with his own children he wasn't able to have. I could hear in his mind how it was all the working and traveling and everything that happened when I was growing up and nobody loving me proper and it was Jaimie too and I was all tired out and my mind was broken and I'd have to go to a looney bin. So I really was like Betty Lou after she jumped off of that barn, after all.

I didn't say one word to Hank. He took me back to our hotel and I could hear the thoughts of people everywhere around me and was about crazy from it, and that night I grabbed any money I had and lit out hitchhiking, and that's why I'm back here near Maple Creek, out in the woods where I know it's safe and there aren't any people around for me to have their thoughts come into my head.

I've been most of my time in this cabin thinking about Jaimie and wanting her here like I never wanted anything in my life. But it can't be, I couldn't stand hearing the thoughts in her head, I'd be taking away from her the only private thing anybody really has. I couldn't do that to her and live.

I got Hank's gun with me, the little pistol he had in case there was trouble he couldn't take care of any other way, and I left him a letter saying mostly what I'm saying on this tape and telling him not to find me and not to have Jaimie try either, if she comes back looking for me. I told Hank I loved him and Polly more than anybody in my whole life and I owed them and Jaimie every happy time I ever had. I don't know that Hank'll show that letter to anybody, he might think it could hurt me if I turned up and wanted to do my singing again.

I couldn't tell him at all where I was heading for because I can't trust him or anybody, not even Jaimie, not to put me in a crazy house like they did to Betty Lou. I can't even think what it'd be like having to listen to the thoughts of people in a crazy house.

I'm staying in these woods, it's all I know to do. This old hunting cabin will do fine for a while, I got some clothes and a supply of food and my ring Polly gave me. And Hank's gun. I figure if I stay here for a time away from everything but the birds and trees and just wait, maybe the voices will go away. It's getting pretty cold, but I figure I can stay here till hunting season starts. I'll go near people when my food runs out and if I still hear the voices I'll leave this tape inside the cabin, and I got Hank's gun to do the rest.

The one thing I don't understand is, I know you all liked my singing. You came out to see me because I was special, because I put something special inside your lives you couldn't put there by yourselves. Other people like me who sing and paint and what all to make you happy — if they knew how you really think about them, they'd stop forever, they wouldn't give you one more thing of themselves.

I've stopped the singing. If the birds in the trees could know about you, they'd stop their singing, too. Whatever happens, I won't ever sing again.

SURVIVOR

She awakened to silence and peace, and whiteness. Blissfully, she floated off again into unconsciousness.

When she awakened once more, the whiteness drifted into focus. The walls were an uneven whitewashed brick. Odd, she thought: no windows. The nightstand was a simple metallic cube, barren of all but an empty glass. The gown and sheet covering her were muslin, wrinkled and musty. The room smelled of cold and dampness and disinfectant.

She lifted her hands from her sides and turned them front and back, examining them with curiosity. They seemed a stranger's hands, dark, puffed up, dry and numb, the fingers hard to bend.

She lay quietly, in profound contemplation of her body. She was very warm — perhaps feverish. But unhurt, she judged.

She struggled to sit up, grimacing at the lassitude of her limbs. Unfamiliar feet dangled beneath her gown, the same dark red color as her hands, possessed of the same puffiness.

Very slowly, she eased herself off the bed. Rocking back and forth, she analyzed the sensations in her feet. They felt, she decided, as if hot water bottles were strapped to them.

Gliding over the floor on her liquid feet, she peered out into a long corridor made of the same coarse brick as her room, a white tunnel extending in both directions into infinity. There was a low murmuring to her left, and she stepped out of her room toward the sound.

Intersecting invisibly only a few feet away was another corridor; and around its corner, seated at a small metal desk, a woman clad in a zippered white jump suit and close-fitting white cap spoke into a headset, her head bent over a clipboard she held in gloved hands. Her nose and mouth were covered by a tight mesh mask.

"Six thousand, sir." Her voice was slightly muffled by the mask. "Estimation thirteen hundred viable. Our last test readings at nine hundred hours, safety range down to oh point one three — Sir?" The woman had looked up. "Excuse me, sir. One of the casualties is here with me. Over and out."

The woman flipped two switches, removed the headset, strode out from behind the desk. She was tall and burly; a few dark hairs straggled from beneath her tight white cap. The eyes above the mask were dark brown, compassionate. "You need to get back to bed."

On a silver nameplate above one breast was the word CAPTAIN; the rest of the name swam and blurred. She reached out for the gray metal desk to steady herself. She could not feel the desk under her hand. "Are you . . . a doctor?" She was shocked by the reedy rasp that was her voice.

"No. Military. Special Forces. I need to get you back into bed." Firmly, the captain took her arm.

"Where am I?"

"The outskirts. Two hundred feet down."

As she walked along the corridor on her warm feet, the captain's guiding hand on her arm, she remembered. The high-low two-note shriek of sirens. The apocalyptic rumble. The sidewalk lurching under her feet. The edges of the building she was running to becoming a shimmer. Then great clouds obscuring everything, and being picked up and slammed down . . .

"Should I talk?" she rasped. "Is it okay to use my voice?"

"Yes," the captain replied softly, "it's okay." Touching her very gently with her gloved hands, the captain helped her into bed, pulled the sheet up.

"I didn't know we had facilities like this."

"You were picked up on our final helicopter reconnaissance."

Sitting on the side of the bed, the captain gazed down at her with moist dark eyes. "We can only tell you the truth. You've been here a few hours. You were wandering in a daze when we found you. You have second and third degree burns over your entire body — "

"But I feel fine!"she uttered.

"Touch your hair."

"What?"

"Do as I say. Touch your hair."

She raised her puffy hands and managed to feel with her fingertips a few bristly patches of hair. "What, what — "

"Burnt off. It's a miracle you have your sight. Most don't. You don't feel anything because your nerve ends are tranquilized by shock. But soon they won't be. And burn pain is the pain of hellfire. Nitric acid has burned into your lungs, that's why your voice is like it is. Soon the sickness will begin. Vomiting, diarrhea, internal bleeding."

The captain reached for her hands, took them into her gloved ones. "Supplies are limited. We have priorities. Broken limbs, reparable injuries. A committee is deciding now on allocation, and difficult decisions will have to be made. You'll require quantities of plasma, antibiotics, sedatives, painkillers. Even with all that, at best estimation you have only a few days to live."

The captain's calm, unpitying eyes stared steadily into hers. She finally said, more to herself than the captain, "I'm eighteen."

"My brother was your age. Davey was in New York." The voice was dispassionate. "Eileen was in New York, too. My lover. We were together thirteen years."

The captain unzipped a pocket of her jump suit, removed a plastic vial, shook a pill into her palm. "This is all we can offer. Supplies of this are the most limited of all. But allocation for you has already been made. Unless, of course, you object on religious grounds."

She extended a cupped hand to the captain. She did not feel the pill that dropped onto her palm.

The captain opened the door of the nightstand, poured a measure of water, barely a mouthful, from a plastic bottle. "Our water supplies are also critical."

"My mother and father, my brothers . . . "

The captain shook her head. "It's been six hours since it all began. All we really know is our major cities are gone."

"A cigarette, could I possibly have a cigarette?"

From another zippered pocket came a pack of Marlboros, a book of matches.

"I'd like to be alone now but . . . I don't want to start a fire."

"Don't worry about that. There's not too much damage to be done down here. Just try your best to put the cigarette in the glass."

"Thank you."

The captain rose, went to the door, turned. She said in her muffled voice, "I suppose you think we're the lucky ones."

The door shuddered, then closed slowly on its air brakes.

There was no sensation of swallowing, only a slight awareness of liquid sliding down her throat.

She lighted the cigarette, took a deep drag, felt something flutter in her lungs. Her head swimming, she dropped the cigarette into the glass where it hissed into extinction.

She lay back and looked at the white walls until they began to waver, then she closed her eyes.

O CAPTAIN, MY CAPTAIN

Lieutenant T. M. Harper applied her fingertips to the printreader at dock area 43, and boarded *Scorpio IV*. A tone sounded within the craft signifying entry; there was no other acknowledgement of her presence.

Disappointed, she realized that of course Captain Drake would be off-ship, taking advantage of the remaining hours before departure. Moon Station 13 might not be Earth, but it had Earth comforts and was staffed with bored military personnel who would welcome the august company of a civilian transport captain. And it was incomparably closer to home than either the captain or herself would be during the next four lonely months. Still, she was puzzled. Transport captains were by nature iconoclastic, and Captain Drake had earned a reputation for extreme reclusiveness.

A few of the readout screens lining the brilliantly lighted command cabin radiated data which Harper ignored, knowing it to be standard orbital information for spacecraft scheduled for departure. She glanced at the chronometer to determine what division of night and day would be operative on *Scorpio IV:* mean Greenwich time. The captain, Harper remembered, was European born. There were four command chairs, regulation for a class one transport, even though only two were needed for the voyages of this particular craft. She had not expected *Scorpio IV* to be different, and it wasn't.

Moving through the galley she looked into the computer room at the standard module and backup, then continued on toward the sleeping cubicles, directing her gear bubble in front of her. She shook her head over the unnatural brightness everywhere, knowing she would have to adjust to it. It was understandable that any transport captain spending months away from the sun's golden warmth would be greedy for bright light . . .

She knew the Captain's more spacious quarters would be at the end of the corridor; she would choose among the remaining three. But she halted at the first doorspace. Its portal was labeled LIEUTENANT HARPER.

Harper gazed in amusement down the corridor. She had been installed the maximum distance from Captain Drake's quarters. Considering all the time the captain spent trapped with unchosen company in this tiny craft, an obsession with privacy was also understandable.

Harper had good reason to doubt that she herself would retain her sanity for very long in such circumstances. She had won her officer's commission on a twelve-person battle cruiser surveillance mission to the Orion sector, had been enthralled by the challenge and adventure of those nine months, had passed the psych probes both during and after the assignment.

But back on the solid footing of Earth, for months afterward she had felt disconnected, her mind — or perhaps her soul — somehow still adrift in those spectacular reaches she had floated through like a weightless seed on alien winds. And she knew from the oblique comments of other members of her officer corps that her experience had not been unique.

She steered her gear into the cubicle, then programmed the doorlock to open to four arhythmic taps of her fingernail. She too would have her privacy.

She stretched tiredly, wishing she could relax on the wide, inviting bunk. Sex with Niklaus last night had been exhausting, as if the two of them had been frenziedly trying to build a storehouse against the parched months ahead. She began to stow her gear.

"Lieutenant Harper, welcome aboard." The low voice resonated like a cello.

Turning, Harper stared, transfixed.

The tall, pale figure in the doorway — dark-haired, clad in black trousers and a high-collared gray shirt — possessed a dramatic beauty so androgynous that Harper could not have guessed her sex unless she had known beforehand.

"Captain Drake," she managed to say, fascinated by the heavy-lidded dark eyes which seemed weary with their burden of intelligence.

"My apologies," Drake said. "I did expect you around this time, it's just that my diurnal rhythms are turned around." The smile was fleeting, but Harper was astonished by its magnetism. "I was resting in my quarters when you came in."

The captain crossed her arms and scrutinized Harper with open interest. "I trust you brought more comfortable garb. I accept your necessary military presence, but I detest military trappings."

Harper glanced down at her Space Service uniform to conceal her ire. The forest green jacket had been hard won and she was proud of it, she was proud of her Lieutenant's silver bar. But if her training and the mission to Orion had taught her nothing else . . . "I brought a few jumpsuits," she conceded.

"Good. I'll look forward to seeing you in them. Departure is confirmed for twenty-one hundred hours. I'll expect you on the bridge for final check at sixteen hundred."

Harper caught herself as her hand began its automatic upward flick toward salute. "Yes, Captain."

Again the brief, magnetic smile. "Call me Drake." And she vanished, moving soundlessly down the corridor.

Drake. So much warmer than Captain. Sourly, Harper pulled a green standard-issue jumpsuit out of her gear. If she doesn't have a first name then neither do I.

* * * * *

As *Scorpio IV* made its leap into hyperspace, Harper slumped exhaustedly in her command cabin chair.

"Get coffee, whatever you like," Drake told her in a tone of dismissal, shutting down all but a dozen of the readout screens. "You've been well trained, Harper, I'm pleased with your technological grasp of my ship."

Harper nodded, watching Drake check course trajectory, her strong, long-fingered hands moving surely over the console, entering data, changing the pattern of the templates.

For the past three hours Harper had been fully absorbed in all the readout screens, occasionally verifying and detailing a status problem for the imperious woman in the command chair beside her, observing with increasing awe Drake's total comprehension and manipulation of swiftly changing computer analyses. Well-versed in the lore of civilian transport captains and their extraordinary hands-on knowledge, she had suspected the stories to be at least somewhat exaggerated — especially the claim that some of these individuals could actually direct a Robomech-four. All military spacecraft were checked and cross-checked by teams of specialists, and specialists had been involved in final systems check of this civilian craft. But Drake had ignored them. She had been as one with her ship, her glance penetrating every analysis on every readout screen simultaneously, and she had directed her own robot repairs and adjustments.

Some military craft had gone out and never returned, their final communications the stuff of legend and nightmare in the Service. Harper knew that if any problem developed on *Scorpio IV,* Drake would know in an instant where it was and how to correct it.

This assignment was a prize. Other officers had been equally qualified to be the military presence on this spacecraft, but hers had been the lucky number to come up. She would be the one to reap all the tangible and intangible benefits when *Scorpio IV* returned with its priceless cargo from the Antares asteroid belt.

She rubbed her eyes; they ached and burned from staring at the readout screens in this too-bright cabin. She smiled, remembering her psych training, all those exercises in negotiating basic incompatibilities during extended space travel. There would be no negotiating with this autocratic woman. Drake possessed irreplaceable ability and the emotional components necessary for remaining sane while she expended the prime years of her life in space. *Scorpio IV* was Drake's home. Harper would be the one to adjust.

But the compensations were handsome. As each day of these next four months passed, credits would be deposited to her account, and when this tour of duty ended she would have three years hazard pay, tax free. When her military obligation was completed she would retire and pursue an Earth-based career, perhaps settle in with the devoted, patiently waiting Niklaus.

She unfastened her restraint and got up. "May I bring you something, Cap — uh, Drake?"

Drake looked at her then, and Harper backed away in
recoil from dark eyes that seemed haunted by grief, as empty
and blasted as a dead star. The voice was soft, and flat:
"Nothing, Harper, thank you."

* * * * *

Knowing better than to presume Drake would wish to
share a mealtime with her, Harper assembled dinner from the
autoserv, paying little attention to her selections. All food
onboard a spacecraft, no matter how it tasted — and most of it
tasted remarkably good — was a synthetic formulation of the
same nutrients. A space crew could dine solely on chocolates
and still eat a balanced diet.

Dutifully consuming her poached trout and vegetable
salad, Harper concentrated on reassembling her
self-assurance. Drake might know every technological
configuration of her spacecraft, she reflected spitefully, but
that did not mean she was a superior being. Rumor had it that
transport captains were psychologically hermitic and sexually
dysfunctional — major reasons why they performed so sanely
and successfully in space.

And the formidable Drake did not, after all, outrank her;
her captaincy was a civilian title, and civilian captains were a
dying breed. Transport craft increasingly were unmanned,
guided by a network of space stations in the civilized universe.
Once another method was found for either harvesting the
Antares asteroid crystals or duplicating them, little work would
be left for a specialist like Drake; she would be reduced to
transporting conventional cargo between the few cultures who
stubbornly continued to demand traditionally manned craft for
commercial transactions.

Drake might be contracted to the great ExxTel
Corporation, but she, Harper, represented the elite Space
Service, the military arm of the most dominant coalition of

corporate, military, and democratic power in the history of Earth. She had been assigned to *Scorpio IV* because she was well qualified to be military liaison on this civilian voyage to the asteroid belt girdling Antares; it was her sole responsibility to monitor the collection and transportation of the asteroid crystals to ExxTel warehousing facilities orbiting Mars.

But still . . . Harper suddenly pushed her food away, grimacing. She knew very well that she was a mere passenger. Only one military liaison had been assigned to this spacecraft because one person with nothing to do was sufficient. She would perform the duties for which she had been meticulously trained only if incapacitating illness or death struck the captain of *Scorpio IV*.

She would then limp this craft into the nearest Space Station — unless the illness or death occurred within the asteroid belt. Rescue within the asteroid belt, if possible at all, would have to be attempted by another transport captain because she, Harper, would be helpless to accomplish it herself. Her prime function on this voyage, she conceded darkly, was the equivalent of a hovering vulture, a cemetery watcher.

Only a transport captain with Drake's skills would dare venture into the Antares asteroid belt which had been claimed indisputably by Earth, nearby civilizations having believed it to be a mysterious, destructive wasteland of drifting rock. Nearly two centuries earlier, twelve military cruisers — nine of them investigative craft — had vanished near Antares without any visual or vocal transmission to provide the faintest clue. The sector had finally been abandoned, written off as the deep space equivalent of the Bermuda triangle, declared off limits to military patrols and transport vessels.

Then ten years ago one of those lost ships, *Pisces II*, perhaps propelled by the effects of a solar flare from the violent Antares, had floated free from the negligible gravity of the asteroid belt, had been picked up on the scanners of civilian transport Captain Reba Morton. All controls and communication equipment in Morton's spacecraft had lost their calibration as she approached the asteroid belt and *Pisces II,* but still she had managed to dock with the dead cruiser and manually guide her craft to a Space Service monitoring station. Only a civilian transport captain like Morton could have overcome the disabling of her own basic robot repair devices and recalibrated the spacecraft's instrumentation sufficiently to accomplish such a feat.

Apparently the crew of *Pisces II,* victims of suicidal madness, had blown themselves out through a hatchlock. And Antares asteroid crystals had drifted in . . . Thus, by purest chance, a vital component of human life on Earth and other Earth-gravity planets had been discovered. Morton and the Space Station crew were the first to experience the wondrous property of the Antares asteroid crystals.

In direct ratio to their size and quantity, the crystals imparted weightlessness. Applications for the crystals were immediately and excitingly obvious in virtually every technological area, especially transportation and medicine. But the greatest clamor was raised by gerontologists. After a century of well-financed research, they had not been able to extend life expectancy beyond one hundred and ten years. Antares asteroid crystals were not the fountain of youth but they represented a dramatic breakthrough, releasing individuals from the wearing, aging effects of standard Earth gravity. Use of the crystals to reduce weight to one-tenth standard gravity could add as much as thirty years to the average human life span.

The drawback was scarcity. For the first time since the twenty-first century, glaring disparity again existed between rich and poor, this time involving not the commodities affecting the quality of life, but the commodity of life itself. The crystals were costly and in continuous demand, due to the difficulty in harvesting them and their perishability: over time their power gradually faded.

Because of their priority-one military applications, the crystals had been rated as strategic materials and placed under the jurisdiction of ExxTel and the Space Service. Token patrols guarded the Antares system at a cautious half-a-light-year distance and in desultory fashion — the gates of heaven could be no less accessible.

In an age of specialization, any spacecraft large enough to transport the many technicians required for recalibrating its disabled systems would be gripped by Antares' gravity, with lethal results. And ExxTel scientists had thus far failed to provide effective shielding against the crystals' effect on a spacecraft's onboard computers and guidance systems. Nor had they made any progress toward duplicating the molecular structure of the crystals, seemingly unique in their defiance of the laws of physics, nor in recreating the environment that would allow them to self-replenish as they did within their home in the Antares asteroid belt.

Only an extraordinarily gifted civilian transport captain like Drake could venture into an asteroid system with spacecraft guidance and communication systems inoperative, and recalibrate those systems without benefit of robot repair or remote command . . .

Feeling a prickling between her shoulder blades, a sensation of being watched, Harper whirled. At the periphery of her vision was a tiny dark fluttering. She blinked once and the fluttering was gone. She blinked again, in annoyance. She had been in deep space a matter of mere hours, it was much too early for mind tricks to begin . . .

Drake walked into the room, her long lean body fluid in its movements. She drew a small tumbler of tomato juice from the autoserv and sipped it standing, her dark, unreadable gaze lingering on Harper.

"You'll have dinner now?" Harper politely inquired.

"Later," answered Drake in her cello tones. She contemplated her tomato juice and smiled, then drained it and disposed of the container. Without another word she left the galley.

Too bone-weary to further speculate about the enigmatic Captain Drake, Harper went off to her quarters, knowing the spacecraft's alarms — or Drake — would awaken her if need be, and no need would be.

* * * * *

Early the next morning Drake was absent from the command cabin. She would be in her quarters, Harper knew, although from what she now understood about the captain, those so-called unusual diurnal rhythms which required daytime sleep were undoubtedly an excuse for avoiding Harper's company.

After receiving a loving transmission from Niklaus over the privacy channel, and dispatching a message back, Harper went up to the observation deck. As she stepped off the ramp she looked around in amazement. Although equipped with the usual library and aural-visual access, the deck was definitely non-standard in its accoutrements. A huge earth-toned body-meld sofa, and two oversize chaises finished in sensuous gold fabric, faced the non-reflective windows. Harper sighed happily.

Except for her meals and an occasional mandatory status review of the spacecraft's basic systems, she spent the day on the deck curled up in the sofa, lost in spectacular coronas, shimmering veils of stardust, the blazing hues of star systems filling the windows.

Around seven o'clock that evening, as Harper finished her bouillabaisse, Drake appeared in the galley. Again Drake wore black pants and another high-collared shirt, this one scarlet. Again Harper was startled by her, unsettled by the masculine elements softened by feminine beauty. Recovering, she said wryly, "Good morning. Ready for breakfast?"

As she had last night, Drake drew a glass of tomato juice from the autoserv. "This will do," she replied expressionlessly. A pale hand resting flower-like on her hip, she sipped her juice. She studied Harper until Harper rose under the intensity of the gaze and disposed of her dinner receptacle.

"I'll be on the observation deck," she told Drake tersely. The psych probes might pronounce Drake sane, but she was *strange*.

"I'll join you shortly," Drake returned.

A tiny gesture of friendliness? Not likely. From the distance of that tone, from the look of the observation deck, Drake simply preferred to be there. Abruptly, Harper took her leave.

Several minutes later Drake entered the deck and reclined on a chaise, gracefully crossing her long legs. She had chosen the chaise across from where Harper sat on the sofa as if she meant to invite conversation, but she turned fully away to gaze out the windows. Harper looked at her with bold resentment. Drake was in her line of vision and disturbed her absorption in the spectacular vistas beyond the windows. And Drake's aloofness, her silence, disturbed for less tangible reasons. As Harper stared at her, she became gradually, unwillingly, absorbed in her.

Drake could be in her thirties or forties — perhaps even her fifties. Her skin, with its luminous, silken pallor, held no sign of age; but the dark eyes, with their weary, almost haunted intelligence, suggested that she had seen altogether too much. Drake's cap of fine dark hair, smoothed back over her ears, curled softly around the nape of her neck and over the top of her collar; a few unruly strands fell over her forehead. Her nose was thin and straight, a slight flare to the nostrils. The lips were cast delicately, the teeth interesting in their slight unevenness. Drake looked like a poetically handsome young man — or a boyish woman of intriguing beauty.

Feeling a pull on her own sexuality, stirred by the remote melancholy of Drake's face, the inviting texture of the dark hair, those strong yet fine hands, Harper reminded herself that Drake's body was the body of a woman. And she had never wished to touch or be touched by a woman. If Drake were a man...

Reminding herself of the patiently waiting Niklaus, Harper reflected that it was not much wonder Drake spent her in-port time cloistered within this spacecraft. Wherever she might venture, her striking beauty and ambiguous sexuality would arrest conversation, would compel attention no matter what the onlooker's sexual proclivities. It was also not much wonder that Drake would hold Harper herself at arm's length; Drake had been forced to endure lengthy contact with a woman in whom she had not the slightest emotional or sexual interest.

This journey, Harper groaned inwardly, would be interminable. She might as well be occupying *Scorpio IV* by herself unless she could somehow break through this woman's wall of isolation by establishing that she had no intention of making any demand of any kind.

She cleared her throat. "I can't imagine ever tiring of this." She gestured toward the windows. "I suppose you must be accustomed to it."

Drake turned to look directly at her. "The pleasure has never lessened."

The intense dark eyes compelled, and seemed suddenly dangerous, as if Harper could be drawn into their depths without possibility of release. Gathering, steeling herself against this disquieting woman, Harper offered, "I'm sure you've made great inroads in the ship's library."

Drake's face softened into a smile. "I've read everything."

Harper quickly recovered herself and smiled back, realizing that Drake was either joking or she had read only within limited fields of interest; there were half a million volumes stored in the spacecraft's memory. "How do you pass the time, then? What do you enjoy?"

"What do I enjoy," Drake repeated. She turned away again, but Harper knew she was contemplating her answer.

"I enjoy this," Drake finally responded, gesturing toward the grandeur beyond the windows. "I enjoy music." She tapped a control on the arm of her chaise, and Harper was immediately chilled by the keenly wrought grief of a solo violin. "And I enjoy . . . taking nourishment."

Harper gaped at her. She had yet to see Drake consume anything but tomato juice. But then in all probability she had installed an autoserv in her quarters. But still . . . Drake was reed slender, her flesh distributed with sparest economy over her tall frame. Autoserv controlled the balance of nutrients in the food taken from its self-replenishing banks, but did not govern the amount of intake; psych probes measured weight gain beyond the individual's established norm as an indicator of psychosis.

Drake was smiling, a maddeningly private smile. Too fascinated to feel resentment, Harper stared at her.

"Something else I enjoy," Drake said, "is learning about the individuals who join me on these voyages. I look forward to hearing about your life."

"That will take twenty minutes," Harper stated, making no pretense at modesty. Her life had taken on color and energy only since she had joined the Service.

Again Drake smiled. "We have one hundred and eighteen days before we achieve final orbit. You have twenty-seven entire years to tell me about between now and then."

"The twenty-seven years just aren't that interesting," Harper insisted, morose with her certainty.

"Perhaps not to you but they will be to me," Drake said in her low expressive tones. Again her intense gaze settled on Harper.

Whatever else Drake might be, Harper realized, she had to be very lonely. She gazed back at Drake. Her beauty seemed even more poetic than before.

* * * * *

For the past hour they had been sitting quietly, listening to a string quartet, watching ever-changing spectacle transmute the view windows.

Drake broke the silence. "Tell me where you were born."

To Harper, the quiet had been companionable; and the question — this particular question — was distinctly unwelcome. "British Columbia," she answered crisply, hoping the unembellished reply would divert Drake to another topic.

Drake flicked a glance at her. "And where in British Columbia?"

Harper sighed. "New Alabama."

The fine, slightly curved brush strokes that were Drake's eyebrows moved upward. "A Trad settlement, is it not?"

"Yes. It's also the large part of my life that's not interesting."

"Your family, are they still there?"

Sighing again, Harper nodded. "They're happy to be there. I'm happy *not* being there. They're ashamed of me. I'm ashamed of them."

Drake got up from her chaise, moved to sit beside Harper. "Tell me about it. Tell me about your parents. Describe them."

She nodded again, less reluctantly. The eyes looking into hers were alert and interested. She could not shut off Drake's first attempt at communication. "My mother is a small woman, my father — "

"No. Describe them in detail. So I can *see* them. So I can see your life with them as well."

Held by Drake's dark gaze, Harper continued obediently, "My mother is fifty-three now. I have her eyes except mine are a lighter blue ... "

Professing interest in the smallest detail of Harper's growing up years, Drake drew out reminiscence, her precise questions opening doors to memory Harper had closed off or forgotten existed. She had managed for the past ten years to avoid discussion and even thought of that pain-filled time when she had defied her parents, when she had scorned the Traditionalist doctrines of the militant settlements which had sprung up more than two centuries ago and to this day continued to attract colonists. The detailed recounting seemed to relieve a deep inner festering, and she spoke more and more willingly.

"It was my great-grandparents who moved there, when Montreal put in its free-trade spaceport. They packed up and left along with thousands of other Quebec families — "

Drake was nodding gravely. "And your own parents inherited all that xenophobia."

"Exactly. They thought an ancient convoluted mess like the Bible was sacred, they were afraid of the real sacredness of the entire living universe. My parents — all the Trads — have a desperate need to control some part of a world that continues to evolve all around them."

"We may dream of an unchanging present and a predictable future," Drake mused, "but real survival comes from adaptation. And the true secret is seeing the exact ways one must adapt ... "

"The settlement finally judged me a non-conformist heretic," Harper continued in a rush of words, almost dizzy with the release of emotion. "But I'd been longing to escape from the time I was small ... "

As she began to describe the childhood dreams of space and freedom which had been awakened by the drama and majesty of the Northern Lights, Drake interrupted her. "Enough for tonight. Tomorrow you can tell me more."

Harper looked at her chronometer in amazement. She had been talking nearly four hours. And suddenly she *was* tired. She was drained.

As she got up from the sofa she asked Drake curiously, "When do you usually turn in?"

"I always retire before six o'clock in the morning."

The next day Harper spent more than an hour in her quarters performing her entire repertoire of physical exercise, then passed the rest of the day on the observation deck, too enthralled with the brilliance beyond the windows to avail herself of the ship's library or any other distraction.

Again Drake appeared in the galley about seven o'clock, wearing a midnight blue shirt with her black pants. Harper realized that if Drake had indeed "retired" to her quarters before six this morning, she had remained there for better than half a standard day.

As Drake drew her usual beverage from the autoserv, Harper welcomed her with a smile. "You do consume something besides tomato juice?" she joked.

Drake looked at her icily. Her voice descended to an even chillier depth: "My personal habits are surely of no consequence."

Don't presume *anything*, Harper raged at herself as she shrugged mute apology. Just because she's interested in your life doesn't mean *anything* beyond that. "Perhaps I'll see you on the deck," she said evenly, and left the galley.

Moments later Drake appeared and sat beside her. Scant minutes afterward Harper was thoroughly immersed in relating memories of her Traditionalist schooling.

"Biblical voodoo," she pronounced in summary dismissal. "Ludicrous beliefs about universe creation and so many other irrationalities — you can't even imagine."

"I can indeed imagine," Drake stated in her resonant tones. "How did you come to question your indoctrination? Most people never do."

There was something besides acute perceptiveness in Drake's eyes — could it be admiration? Harper answered self-consciously, "The settlement's computers used data lockout, naturally. But anyone with half a brain could figure out how to bypass them and get into Earth's major libraries. I had half a brain."

"So you educated yourself. Enough to qualify for the Space Service. Amazing."

Admiration, definitely it was admiration in Drake's eyes. Warm with pleasure, Harper shrugged. "Not quite. I spent too much time indulging in novels, especially the famous ones from the nineteenth and twentieth centuries. I had to take potentiality tests and was lucky enough to finish in the top percentile for scientific aptitude. The Service's own institutions completed my education to Service specification."

"Tell me more," Drake said. "Tell me what you remember about the potentiality tests."

Why was she so interested in all this, Harper wondered. No one in her entire life had ever been interested in these nooks and crannies of her life. She said, "We've talked only about me. I'd like to know about you."

Drake shook her head, her eyes suddenly distant, shuttered.

Harper held out her hands in placating gesture. "Just a few basic questions. Like where you were born."

"In a village outside Bucharest. I want to hear the answer to my question about the tests."

"How old are you?" Harper persisted.

The slow rise and fall of Drake's shoulders clearly conveyed her inaudible sigh. She looked away, out the windows. "Eight hundred and twenty-two," she replied. "If I want to talk about myself, I will. I don't."

Then neither do I, Harper wanted to retort. But the desire was too strong to experience again what this woman had given her last night — the new and highly pleasurable sensation of someone consumingly interested in her.

She answered Drake's question. She answered many more questions about her education until late into that night, until Drake again sent her off to bed exhausted and emotionally depleted from the effort of recapturing the minutia of her life.

* * * * *

Over the next weeks Harper's waking hours fell into routine: the required systems monitoring and standard transmissions to Space Service Trade Liaison Headquarters; her meals and exercise regimen; exchanging communications with Niklaus; the observation deck. The hours were also spent in restless anticipation of Drake's appearance in the galley and the long, intense evening that would follow.

Drake had, Harper admitted, become an addiction. Worse than that, with each successive evening Drake's physical magnetism was pulling her ever further into its grip. The magnetizing force, she supposed, was Drake's androgynous beauty, but whatever the causative factor, what difference did it make? She was beguiled by the pale, idyllic beauty of that face, the profound intelligence of those eyes absorbing every single word she uttered.

It was absurd. And hopeless. And demeaning. Not to mention paradoxical. Drake had lavished hours of her time and the complete focus of her mind on Harper, yet had relinquished not one iota of her essential being. The spiteful speculation Harper had indulged in a month ago about Drake being sexually dysfunctional seemed only too correct: Drake's sensual response was given entirely to music and the beauty of the galaxy. Harper longed to touch that austere face, to reach some answering inner chord. But she could come no closer to Drake than she could to those stars beyond the view windows. And like those stars, Drake's hard beauty served to attract and then inflame anything venturing near . . .

In only these few weeks Niklaus had slipped from her thoughts, the daily message to him containing merely dutiful affection. She comforted herself that he would be there, loving and faithful, when she returned from this voyage, whereas Drake would be gone from her forever, a part of the coldly brilliant stars . . .

The sumptuous romanticism of a flute concerto filled the observation deck. Harper sat on the sofa, waiting, staring at Drake who reclined on her chaise, a hand on her knee, absorbed in the spectacular hues of reflection nebulae shimmering over a vast open star cluster — the same star system Harper had watched throughout her solitary afternoon. Finally Drake turned from the view windows, and Harper knew with a surge of excitement that the evening would now begin.

"Tell me about your friends," Drake said, getting up and moving toward her. "What are they like?"

"I'm pretty much a loner," Harper confessed, stirred by the litheness of the body within the white shirt and black pants. "A few people I'd term good buddies, the rest are just acquaintances."

"Sexual awareness," Drake said, sitting beside her. "When did that begin?"

It was a first venture into this subject area, and after mild surprise Harper decided that Drake was simply filling in blanks.

"Sexual awareness," she repeated, and grinned. "Probably around the age of seven. When I first understood that my gravest responsibility was preservation of my virginity. I got rid of the thing when I was twelve."

Harper was pleased; she had made Drake laugh before, but rarely.

Drake said, smiling, "You had many dreams when you were growing up. What were your sexual dreams?"

Suddenly and inexplicably uncomfortable, Harper took refuge in generality. "I dreamed mostly of sexual freedom. Of never being in a stifling relationship like my parents had. Escaping all those sexual rules assigned by the Trads . . . "

"Yes, but what kind of relationship, what kind of person did you dream of finding?"

Harper stiffened against discussing any of the men she'd chosen to be with, any of those emotionally sterile relationships. "I've always walked away from anyone who tried to interfere with what I wanted to do with my life."

"From what I know of you," Drake murmured, "I'd be very surprised if you didn't. When you were growing up, you surely dreamed of a sexual ideal. What was that ideal?"

Drake's dark gaze held her, pierced her. If she had ever before met someone who looked like Drake . . .

"I . . . " Harper searched for coherent thought. Her nipples tingled almost painfully into hardness, she felt heat within her thighs. "A gentle and very tender . . . friend."

"Who looked like . . . "

"Dark hair," she uttered, feeling the heat rise to her face. "Dark eyes." She tried to look away from Drake but could not, and knew that the desire closing up her throat was naked on her face.

Drake's hands taking hers — the first touch between them — unraveled her.

"What else." The eyes were mesmerizing, the voice hypnotic.

Harper swayed toward her as if bent by a wind. "A face ... like yours."

Drake's hands released hers to grip her shoulders, to draw Harper to her.

Stunned, her body hammered by heartbeats, Harper slid her unbelieving arms around the slender body. Drake lowered her to the sofa, her lips a feather-light brushing of Harper's face. Harper arched as Drake's mouth came to her throat, as a velvet tongue began to stroke. She seized Drake's hair, imprisoned Drake's head between her hands and greedily absorbed with her lips the warm silk, the sculptured planes of the face so miraculously in her possession.

Drake's mouth sought hers, took hers. Harper slid her hands under Drake's shirt, then made a single sound as Drake's tongue entered her. Drake's hands momentarily held her face, then slid down to her throat, the fingertips caressing. Then Drake pulled open Harper's jumpsuit, held her bare shoulders.

Melted by the slow strokes of Drake's tongue, Harper shuddered under the hands that moved slowly down over shoulders to her breasts. The hands cupped firmly, the fingers immediately beginning a rhythmic rippling of her swollen flesh. Drake's mouth finally left hers to come again to her throat, and Drake's hands on her breasts squeezed, released, squeezed, released, until her breasts felt like bursting fruit. Drake slid her hands under her and clasped her hips. Then her nipples became a fierce sweet ache in Drake's mouth as Drake's hands on her hips squeezed, released, squeezed, released.

Drake raised her body and spread Harper's thighs fully open to kneel between them. Harper felt her wetness on

Drake's palm, then writhed from the fingers that stroked her open. Overpowered by her need, she groaned as the fingers left her, watching feverishly as Drake brought those fingers to her mouth, tasted them.

"Oh so very lovely and so very wet." Drake's voice was thick, her heavy-lidded eyes an unfocused darkness of pleasure.

Then Drake was bending over her and Drake's fingers were sliding into her and filling her and Harper's hips rose as she closed rigidly around them. With a low moan Drake moved down to her. Drawing swift breaths, Harper gasped her ecstasy as the fingers stroked, the velvet tongue stroked. Stroked and stroked and stroked her to an incandescence of orgasm.

Drake eased her fingers from her. Weakly, Harper wound her fingers in Drake's hair to take her mouth away, but Drake grasped her hands, preventing her.

"I can't . . . again," Harper whispered, "not . . . after that. Not . . . for a while."

Drake took her mouth away. Her voice came in a murmur, from deep in her throat: "This next voyage will be as long as you could possibly wish." Her mouth came back to Harper, her tongue slid into her, began a slow circling.

Harper flung her hands up over her head, her body undulant, a rolling wave of desire spreading all the way up into her throat. She wanted the velvet tongue everywhere, endlessly.

A timeless interval later, Harper felt her body being lifted, carried, lowered into a place of blissful darkness. She was aware of a fluttering sound, a whisper of breeze. Then she became part of the darkness.

* * * * *

Awakening in her quarters, Harper rolled over and stretched in delicious, unthinking languor before she realized her nudity and the origin of her contentment.

It was late morning, her status confirmation report was due in shortly to Headquarters. She could not, as she usually did, wake up in leisurely fashion and use this first hour for her exercise regimen. Not that she needed exercise, she reflected wryly, not after her body had been so continuously and exquisitely wracked by sexual tension unlike anything she had ever known . . .

She climbed reluctantly out of bed, longing to have this time undisturbed to sort through the confusion of her thoughts.

Smoothing back the tangles of her hair, she smiled mockingly at her visage in the reflective wall of her quarters. So Drake was sexually dysfunctional, was she? If Drake had been any less dysfunctional, she, Harper, would not have survived the night.

Marveling at the euphoric lightness of her limbs, she examined herself from head to foot. She looked no different. Her body was its usual trim shape; there was no mark anywhere to signify any alteration in her. Yet there had been an alteration; she felt tangibly changed.

Cupping her breasts, she leaned closer to her reflection. The nipples were heightened in color; and they budded into hardness as she remembered how they had been savored in Drake's mouth. She inspected herself further: her vulva was an even more enhanced shade of pink. Heat flooded her along with memory, and colored all the surfaces of her skin.

Hastily she pulled on a jumpsuit, other memories of the night filtering into her. Drake had remained clothed; Harper had managed only to open her shirt. The breasts within that shirt had been small, their flesh soft and tender to her fingers, the nipples large, their firmness a constant whenever Drake's body had lain on hers. She had not been able to kiss those breasts. She had not been able to kiss or touch Drake intimately anywhere. Drake had completely overpowered her.

Tonight all that would change.

* * * * *

As the morning ended and the afternoon wore on, as Drake did not appear, Harper's mood plummeted from anticipation to depression, then veered off into anger. Drake had been the initiator of last night's passion, the pure aggressor throughout. Therefore, by all logic it had been meaningful to her. And therefore she could have — should have — made an exception to her rigid routine and left her quarters to be with Harper. Harper had surrendered herself, Drake should understand that she *needed* the assurance of Drake's presence during this vulnerable aftermath . . .

To hell with her, Harper decided, and stalked off to her quarters. But as seven o'clock neared she could not remain there. She compromised by going up to the observation deck instead of to the galley.

Shortly afterward, when Drake entered the deck and walked to her chaise, Harper did her best to ignore her. Drake settled herself and did not speak; she did not look at Harper. Her eyes were distant and shrouded, as if their focus had turned entirely inward.

Harper looked at her in a fury of frustration. What could possibly be in this woman's unfathomable mind? What could the reason be for her unfathomable behavior? Nothing in the experience of her own life or in any fictional life she had ever read could account for this unique, inexplicable, utterly maddening woman.

She was struck by the thought that Drake was feeling her own vulnerability. Drake had no choice about who accompanied her on her voyages, but by the pitiless dictates of her lonely profession, she also had no choice — whatever her libido — about resisting a futureless emotional involvement with any of her passengers. If Drake had restrained herself behind a carefully constructed wall of self-protection, this would explain her hungered, tireless passion last night, and her withdrawal now . . . For that matter, it would explain *all* of Drake's behavior.

Buoyed by this possibility, Harper managed a smile and a neutral tone. "A month ago when you listed what you enjoyed, you didn't mention lovemaking."

Drake seemed to emerge from her self-absorption with effort. Her answering smile was slow and luminous. "Did I not?"

Momentarily disassembled by the renewed potency of Drake's beauty, Harper recovered herself and plunged ahead. "Last night — "

She was startled by the keening of an alarm.

"Code Two." Drake was already on her feet.

Following her from the deck, Harper was grateful that the two-note wail was not the continuously shrilling Code One signifying a major magnitude crisis. But this alarm was different from the other coded alarm signals periodically sounding throughout the craft, benign notifications of gravity force fluctuations or requests for fail-safe confirmation of course changes, routine matters which Drake could and did monitor without emerging from her quarters. This alarm was ominous.

In the command cabin Drake swept a single glance over the monitor screens and announced tersely, "Breech in the aft deflection shield. It's widening."

The Code Two alarm became a Code One continuous shrill. Harper felt the hair rise on back of her neck. The shields were the vital energy force that protected the craft's surface. A breakdown could leave *Scorpio IV* exposed to a lethal bombardment of space debris . . .

Drake said, "Call up Robomechs AZ-niner-two and three. Robomech-four on standby."

Harper flung herself into her seat and initiated the start-up programs that would activate the robots. Drake had already cleared three screens and was leaning over the console, tapping keys. Then she stood with one hand on a hip, the other poised over the console, watching schematics flash past at split-second speed.

The hand over the console pounced, striking a key. "There, right there," she said with satisfaction. She continued to tap the key, rapidly magnifying a diagram and then freezing it on the center screen. "It's bad. The entire shield function is breaking down."

"Can it be repaired?" Harper was astonished by the calmness of her voice.

"Yes. I'll need Robomech-four."

"Right."

If the crisis had needed any further underscoring, the need for Robomech-four had accomplished it.

Her head ringing from the Code One alarm, Harper entered the priority overrides that would channel all but basic life support computer functions into Robomech-four. Then she sat back. She had once observed in a laboratory setting the robot's dissection of the radioactive heart of a military cruiser's stardrive, three highly skilled technicians working in perfect synchrony to correlate and direct its awesome activities. There was no additional assistance she could possibly provide to Drake.

For the next hour she watched in rapt fascination as Drake, standing, her elegant body a stillness of tension, her eyes narrowed in concentration on the color changes transforming the frozen diagram on the center screen, worked the Robomech-four with nerveless surgical precision.

Finally, blessedly, the alarm cut off. Drake said distractedly, "Bring up Robomech-two for routine finish."

Minutes later, at a nod from Drake, Harper terminated all the robot programming sequences, returned the computer to its normal functioning.

She turned to Drake, words of relief and admiration on her lips. But she was unaware of the words she spoke; she was staring at the first clear, readable emotion she had seen in Drake's face: exhilaration.

"You didn't mention another item on that list of what you enjoy," Harper told her. "You love using your ability."

Drake said gravely, "It is the one acceptable power I have."

Harper watched the exhilaration fade from Drake's face. She stared into the depths of the dark eyes, chilled to see again what she had first seen weeks ago: emptiness, a haunted grief.

Drake looked away from her. "Come back to the observation deck," she said softly.

Moments later, Harper waited in indefinable, trembling expectancy as Drake sat on the sofa beside her.

Drake said, "Last night is between us now. But I want our time together to continue as before. I want you to talk to me as before."

Frustrated to the verge of tears by the riddle of this woman, Harper whispered, "I can't."

Drake sighed. "Flowers accept rain without questioning its source or meaning. Is it so difficult to simply accept what happens between us until our voyage ends?"

Harper said bitterly, "So last night you were the heaven-sent rain falling on me."

"Not heaven-sent," Drake replied evenly.

"Last night had no meaning to you?"

"To me it means that there is more between us now."

Harper said vehemently, "I need something from you. *Something.*"

"I can give only what I am able to give."

"What you're *willing* to give."

"For me it is the same."

Harper closed her eyes and turned away from her.

"Talk to me if you can," Drake said gently. "For a while. Will you, Harper?"

She thought in despair, I can either continue with her as before or try to stay away from even the sight of her for the next three and a half months. "All right," she sighed. "What do you want me to talk about tonight?"

"I think . . . places where you lived after you left the Trads. The houses, the cities."

She could not afterward remember what she had been saying when the pale beautiful face neared hers, filling her vision. Only that she had faltered into silence, a brushfire of desire enveloping her.

Then Drake's lips were caressing her face. But with all her strength she held Drake away, she took the gray shirt in her hands and opened it. "I want to see you."

Drake allowed her only briefly to gaze at the long sweeping lines of her body, the lean thighs, the delicate black triangle between. Then Drake's mouth came to hers and Drake took off Harper's jumpsuit. And Harper's body was covered by silk of such astonishing softness and warmth that she could scarcely breathe. Could she possibly feel like this to Drake? Could some other woman possibly feel as Drake did to her?

Drake's unhurried, exploring hands added new dimension to her desire and intensified it. Holding Harper's face, kissing her, she drew Harper's tongue into her and circled its tip. Body memory of the night before returned with such force that Harper surged into her, desire flaring into passion. She moaned her want but Drake pressed the softness of her body sinuously into her and her tongue began another slow rhythm that brought other body memory, fresh and paralyzing. Wrapping her arms and legs around Drake, fused to the nirvana of her body, Harper abandoned herself to Drake's will, to an eroticism that became the very edge of orgasm.

Sometime later Drake moved down between her legs and the edge of orgasm became its measureless fiery heart.

Harper again found herself lifted, carried, lowered.

She clung to Drake. "Stay with me," she mumbled.

"I cannot."

"Till I sleep . . . "

And then she was asleep.

* * * * *

In the next two weeks Harper's existence fell into a disjointed pattern. Service Headquarters had demanded extensive debriefing in order to perform their own analysis of the deflection shield failure and activation of Robomech-four; and with point-of-no-return only thirteen days hence, they had placed go-ahead for the voyage on standby.

"Cupidity, duplicity, stupidity . . . " Harper muttered the same litany of imprecations every morning as she pulled her unwilling body out of bed to oversee transmission of yet another mass of data on *Scorpio IV's* status. Certainly she and Drake would continue this voyage and load their precious cargo of Antares asteroid crystals — and those officious morons at Headquarters knew it. The shield failure had merely given them license to subject her to the bureaucratic minutiae that brightened their tedious, gravity-bound lives.

However unnecessary and monotonous her increased workload might be, she was grateful for its minor distractions. Her unoccupied hours without Drake stretched out blankly, interminably. She consumed her meals with indifference and because she knew she must. She passed the rest of her time meticulously grooming herself, or in dreaming contemplation of the blazing universe beyond the view windows, her mind burning with its own images, her memories of Drake.

With each successive evening, as Drake appeared on the observation deck, she seemed more dramatically beautiful, more dynamic, powerful, magnetizing. With each successive evening Harper succumbed more compliantly to the whims and dictates of Drake's mind, divulging any detail of her life that would hold Drake's complete focus — all of it a part of the waiting for the moment when Drake would reach for her, when she would slide the clothing over Harper's shoulders, when the purest part of the night would begin.

She had tried to give back some measure of her ecstasies one evening before Drake's hands and mouth once more turned her into flame. "This," Drake had told her, her eyes smoldering as she again drew Harper to her, "is everything I require."

In the small part of herself still capable of objective thought, Harper knew desperately that along with her body she was yielding her will, her identity, perhaps even her mind. She had become a voluptuary in thrall to her nightly consummations in Drake's arms, thinking of no past beyond the bliss of the night before, of no future beyond the night ahead. It was small comfort that each night Drake's own passion did not cease until Harper lay in insensate repletion. She was Drake's sexual pawn.

On that earlier voyage to Orion she had been subtly but profoundly affected by the alien vastness of space. Could this be a different manifestation of that same neurosis? After entry into the Antares asteroid belt, when Drake was fully involved with the problems of bringing back to life a disabled *Scorpio IV* — perhaps then she could establish some sort of grip on her saner self . . .

* * * * *

As *Scorpio IV* approached within a light year of the Antares asteroid belt, Service Headquarters signaled its go-ahead just as Harper had known it would. Rendezvous would occur at twenty-hundred hours.

Harper pulled on the close-fitting white coverall she would wear in zero gravity, apparel designed to adhere to any surface of the ship and prevent her from floating as helplessly as a dust mote. Like all Space Service recruits, she had undergone extensive periods of sensory deprivation, and her deep space training had also included weightlessness, a curious and amusing oddity when experienced short-term, but which had produced severe physical and psychological trauma in space age pioneers during the first interplanetary voyages.

She moved awkwardly toward the command cabin, irrationally annoyed by the pull on the soles of her feet, the slowness of her progress. She was well aware of the source of her ill-temper: there would be no lovemaking this night — and subsequent nights as well; Drake would be fully occupied with the navigational challenges of her spacecraft.

Drake was seated in her command chair, eyes fixed on the narrow navigation windows that revealed the Antares asteroid belt, a glowing necklace illuminated by its far distant but spectacularly fiery mother star. Like Harper, Drake also wore a coverall, hers black.

"Only minutes remain for any additional transmissions," Drake stated without looking at her.

"Right," Harper acknowledged, forgiving the officious tone; Drake was immersed in computations for final approach. Before the forces in the asteroid belt could play havoc with the spacecraft's guidance systems, Drake would fully shut down its power and make use of the remaining forward thrust to drift them into a thick, crystal-rich segment of the belt. All was in readiness for the period when she and Drake would be in partial sensory deprivation and dependent on the ship's accumulated oxygen, when *Scorpio IV* would be the equivalent of a dead, drifting shell.

Having earlier completed her transmissions, including one to Niklaus, Harper now sat in quiet excitement that contained a thrill of fear. On the screens she watched each storage hatch slowly flex open in preparation for receiving the asteroid crystals; she watched through the navigation windows the unfolding drama of their approach.

Drake's calm voice penetrated the quiet: "Ten seconds to full shut down." She pulled a light mesh body restraint across herself, as did Harper.

Even though she knew, had been fully trained to expect it, Harper was stunned by the bright cabin's plunge into blackness. Then the utter silence — the silence, she thought, of the grave. Her straining eyes slowly adjusted; finally the orange-red, fluorescin-imbued room emerged into dim, eerie visibility. Drake's body in its black coverall was part of the darkness, but her face was a pale oval in the ghostly white light cast by Antares. The silence quickly became an aching in Harper's ears and she sucked in her breath to hear its sound.

A sigh of satisfaction came from Drake. "Not a trace of yaw."

"I'm glad," Harper said fervently, recoiling from the thought of *Scorpio IV* pitching continuously from side to side throughout all the hours of free fall.

"You should be," Drake said drily. "You'd be throwing up by now."

I suppose you wouldn't, Harper thought, more amused than annoyed by Drake's arrogance. Her white-sleeved arm was floating in front of her; she steered it to the console and smiled as she tried to make her fingernails drum; the hand kept floating upward. Her pre-eminent physical sensation was the adhesive clothing and restraint mesh holding her body into her chair.

She stared out the navigation windows as *Scorpio IV* closed swiftly on the glowing asteroid belt. Their blind, silent spacecraft could as well be one of those aerodynamic paper airplanes she had constructed as a child and cast into the air currents. She continued to watch in speechless awe as the mysterious asteroid belt slowly gathered her and Drake into its radiance and swallowed them whole, as they became part of a thickening world of swirling blue-white crystal, brilliantly glittering jewels colliding soundlessly, harmlessly, against the surfaces of the ship.

"Drake ... " Harper breathed.

"Yes. It is truly beautiful."

Drake's voice came from above her; she had risen to stand beside Harper in the spectral darkness. Drake's face seemed to float beside her as she leaned down to unfasten Harper's restraint. "For now nothing can be done for my ship. Come to me," she said softly, and took Harper's hands.

Her mouth dry, Harper allowed herself to be pulled out of her chair and into Drake's arms, against the substantiality of her body. "Some of our senses need not be deprived," Drake murmured, and her mouth came to Harper's.

She became ever weaker in Drake's arms, immobilized by the swift thrusts of Drake's tongue. Drake opened Harper's coverall, began to slide it from her. Staring into the austere, ethereally beautiful face so close to hers, her pulse pounding in her ears, Harper yielded to what she knew would be ultimate helplessness.

Naked, held to Drake only by a clasped hand, floating like an air bubble, she watched her white clothing drift away somewhere into the black.

Drake pulled Harper to her, clasped Harper's body to hers. Drake had not removed her coverall but had opened it to expose her body; and Harper felt only the exquisite surface contact of Drake's silken skin, felt her breasts only as they touched the warm softness of Drake, as they were caressingly held in Drake's hand; she felt her lips only as Drake savored them, felt her mouth only from Drake's tongue inside her. As Drake's fingers slid slowly, tantalizingly over her thighs and then between her legs, she felt her wetness on Drake's fingers, felt her weightless body swell in a ripening of desire that became a strange, new, keenly throbbing ache.   *

Murmuring thickly, indecipherably, Drake moved Harper's body away from her so that it again floated free. She captured Harper's hips, raised Harper to her mouth.

All feeling in her entire body was focused between her legs, fused to the slow tongue strokes, each a lightning strike of sensation. In the red-etched, black command cabin she writhed uncontrollably, helpless as a windblown flame.

"Please," she gasped, "oh please . . . "

But the strokes only gradually quickened. Anchored to Drake's merciless mouth, her gyrating body rose above Drake's head and then fell back down, then rotated from side to side. She felt the wetness pour from her as Drake's mouth became more avid. She approached a brilliance of orgasm as if she would fall into a star. And then the brilliance consumed her.

Harper was drawn down, into Drake's arms. "So beautifully wonderfully wet . . . ' " Drake's voice was an intoxicated whisper.

Soon afterward Drake held her against a wall, Harper's feet floating off the floor. "The human body is a miracle," Drake murmured, her warm face buried in Harper's breasts. "In new circumstances its nerve paths simply seek new connections . . . " Sometime later she floated Harper free from the wall, and again lifted her. Her tongue inside the writhing, moaning Harper, Drake moaned her own joy.

Harper awakened disoriented, then quickly realized that she was still in the command cabin. Drake, she remembered, had placed her naked in a chair, lowering the chair's back. Her clothing was beside her, the restraint mesh around her. She could not see that Drake was gone, but knew infallibly that she was, that she would be in her own quarters.

She donned her coverall, made her awkward, painstaking way through the eerie fluorescence to her quarters, to the galley; then she returned to the command cabin and the chair where Drake had left her.

Cloaked by the darkness, soothed by it, she removed her coverall and again fastened herself down with the restraint mesh. She stretched sensuously. So this was sensory deprivation. If the Space Service bureaucrats could see her now . . .

With no sense of time passing she gazed contentedly, languorously at the jewel-laden world swirling beyond the windows, its treasures drifting unawares into the ship's storage containers. She wondered if she could have dreamed her memories, those impossible sensations of the night before.

Drake spoke her name from across the room. "How very lovely you look," she added, amusement in her soft tones.

How can she possibly see me from where she is, Harper wondered, straining to make out any image of her. And then the thought passed from her as Drake reached her, bent down to unfasten the restraint. Harper floated up and into her arms.

Drake murmured, "We have only a few more hours . . . Then I must take care of my ship . . . "

Harper learned that she had not dreamed any of the sensations of the night before.

* * * * *

Working from the lowest possible power generation, her hands translucent over the faintly illuminated, blinking console, Drake slowly built up data and set data locks, correlating larger and larger segments into the exponentially expanding design that would bring *Scorpio IV* back to life. Harper, sitting beside her in bemused incomprehension, responded to an occasional tersely worded order and performed the equivalent of handing an implement to an architect.

As the hours passed, as Drake became more immersed in the complexities of her work, her orders ceased. Harper dozed fitfully in her chair, then slept.

The leaden weight of her body and the painfully bright command cabin lights awakened her. Feeling pressed into her chair, she squeezed her watering eyes shut. When she was able to focus, the chronometer told her it was mid-morning. Beside her Drake continued to work, seemingly unaffected by the renewed gravity and light; but her face was drawn, etched in concentration and exhaustion.

Harper asked in concern, "Is there something I can — "

"Yes. Either I calibrate the major systems at one sitting or I must begin all over again. Leave the bridge immediately. Do not return unless I signal for your assistance."

Smarting with anger and humiliation, Harper made her way to her quarters. She donned normal clothing, then wrathfully stalked up to the observation deck. She watched, standing with her arms crossed, the swarming crystals. Her eyes burning from the endlessly varied bright patterns, her injured feelings unsoothed, she sat down on Drake's chaise and distracted herself with *Jane Eyre* from the ship's library.

It was late in the afternoon when a slight vibration under her feet became a hum and gathered strength; the ship's stardrive was beginning its rise to full capacity. Unwillingly, and only as a matter of what she perceived to be her military duty, she marched down the ramp and looked in unobserved on Drake. She gaped in astonishment.

Drake was slumped over her console, her feebly moving hands clawlike, her face deathly pale. Gone were all traces of her magnetism, her power, her overwhelming beauty. She looked gaunt and debilitated, as if she had aged decades.

Harper blurted her shock. "Drake — "

"Leave me." The words were hissed and vehement. "Our lives depend on it."

Harper climbed numbly up to the observation deck. Astonished and terrified, chilled to her marrow with the realization that she might actually have to fulfill her ultimate mission on this voyage, she scanned the status monitors.

All systems were approaching readiness, she saw with relief. Communications were still down, but contact with Headquarters was not essential if it fell on her shoulders to bring *Scorpio IV* out of the asteroid belt and to safety. After she cleared the danger zone she could simply trigger a signal that would pinpoint their position and effect rescue of herself and Drake.

She comforted herself with the likelihood that Drake's illness, serious as it appeared, was acute exhaustion curable by sheer release from the massive outpouring of physical and psychic energy necessary to achieve the resurrection of *Scorpio IV*. Since Drake's diurnal habits and patterns indicated her need for a lengthier restorative period than for most individuals, she had perhaps been doubly affected by this violation of her bodily needs . . .

As Harper sat in quiet analytical assessment of what she had just witnessed, her senses suddenly sharpened into alertness. Warily, she got up from the sofa. Later she would not be certain if she had heard a sound over the rising hum of the stardrive, or if a depth of extrasensory awareness had compelled her to the observation deck ramp.

Drake, her back to Harper, was in the corridor below. Sagging against the wall, she lurched toward her quarters, her black-clad figure doubled over by the agony of her effort, a straining hand sliding along the wall as if groping there for support.

Harper had taken several automatic steps down the ramp before the rigidity of Drake's posture, the desperate, granite determination of her struggle, told Harper that any attempt at assistance would be rebuffed with greater fury than any of her earlier offers of help. Drake had ordered her away unless signaled, and Drake had only to touch the chronometer on her wrist to summon her. But still, from the look of her . . . Uncertain, Harper waited at the top of the ramp, anxiously watching, poised to run.

Just before Drake reached the open portal of Harper's quarters, she paused, straightened with shuddering effort, craned to look within.

She thinks I might be in there. She doesn't want me to see her.

Then Harper saw Drake's black-clad figure crouch. Saw her body seem to contract, to dissolve into a nebulous dark bulk that shrank precipitously. Saw a small creature with sharply pointed, membranous wings gather itself and flutter weakly, erratically down the corridor.

At the portal to Drake's quarters the creature extended its wings fully, flapped once, twice, and became the crouching, collapsing Drake. The portal to Drake's quarters opened to reveal a blackness deep as liquid ink. Drake was absorbed into the blackness, the portal sealing behind her.

Her legs unable to hold her, Harper sank down onto the ramp.

If she needed clear evidence that she had lost even a tenuous grip on reality, here was the proof. Her body might survive this voyage, but her sanity had disintegrated.

Climbing shakily to her feet, Harper managed to reach the sofa where she again collapsed. She stared out into the blue-white crystals, their volatile swirling like the maelstrom within her. She focused on controlling her breathing, on reducing the rapid thudding of her heart. Then she concentrated on seeking some coherency of thought.

Whence had come such bizarre hallucinations? Perhaps she had never really recovered from a childhood filled with tales of the hell-spawned demons the Trads blamed for every evil in the universe. Or perhaps this was a manifestation of her preferred childhood reading — scary goblins and dragons and assorted ghouls.

She gazed at the library fax, still lighted from her earlier reading, a solace to her emotional tumult. There was rationality of one kind on this ship: the rigorous, unchanging printed word.

A superlatively controlled and rational woman like Drake surely would not welcome among her half million volumes any texts relating to Earth folklore. But perhaps there were general references, perhaps she could trigger some memory that would help trace the threads of this psychosis . . .

Harper entered:

Earth folklore
Werewolves, ghouls.

Unable to make her fingers transcribe the one word that was emblazoned in her mind, she added:

And all related entries.

The library responded:

All subject entries cross-referenced to major heading:
Vampires.

The hair rose on the back of Harper's neck. With a tremor she entered:

Display major heading.

The library responded:

Major heading: Vampires
14729 entries
Designate desired sequence.

Again Harper collapsed on the sofa. After a lengthy period of slow breathing to reduce a measure of her panic, she entered:

Vampires, classic characteristics.

Afterward she used a longer period of slow breathing, lying back on the sofa and closing her eyes to marshal all her resources. Then she sat up and considered what she had learned, and her observations of Drake and her ship.

Vampire legend held that the creatures could transform themselves into certain animal forms, most classically into bats. Aside from today's inconceivable events, she had seen a fluttering shape her first night on board, and after lovemaking with Drake had again heard fluttering and even felt the sensation of a breeze — impossibilities on a spacecraft.

Drake had been able to see her with the ship plunged into darkness. Darkness was the natural habitat of the vampire, and Drake spent better than half of each twenty-four hour period enclosed in her quarters. Drake's quarters were pitch black.

The unnatural brightness of *Scorpio IV* resulted in no shadows anywhere from any object, any individual. Masterful concealment for a vampire — because vampires did not cast a shadow.

Vampires could not be about in the daytime without severe diminishing of their powers, and they would die in direct exposure to the sun. Drake's demand for solitude as her strength and powers waned, her desperate struggle to reach the safety of her quarters — all had occurred in what would be late afternoon, Earth-time, and in proximity of a major star, Antares.

Vampires did not reflect an image in a mirrored surface. Except in Harper's own quarters, there were no reflective surfaces of any kind on the ship. Anywhere.

Vampires could be the most hypnotically erotic of creatures, but they did not require conventional sex. They did not eat conventional food; the bloodlust of feeding completely satisfied all bodily and erotic urges . . .

Harper sat perfectly still. *What do you enjoy,* she had asked Drake. And Drake had answered: *I enjoy . . . taking nourishment.*

Harper fled to her quarters, frenziedly ripping off her clothing as she ran. Again and again she scrutinized every inch of her skin in the reflective wall. There were no marks anywhere, none at all.

Her relief was only momentary. If Drake fit other classic criteria, why would she seek prolonged sexual encounters without fulfillment of her need for blood? It made no sense. Maybe, Harper thought dismally, maybe she had conjured everything — including her physical experiences, all those hours in Drake's arms. No. That was impossible. Hallucinating was one thing, but she could not possibly have imagined the ecstasies of Drake's passionate mouth on her, those very specific memories.

Wait a minute. She *had* seen Drake in the act of consuming food . . .

Still naked, she raced from her quarters to the galley. She drew a container of tomato juice, and with a shaking hand smelled the contents. With a relieved sigh she dipped in a finger, then stopped as the dripping finger neared her lips. Autoserv could form specific ingredients to taste and smell like any number of foods. This tomato juice might yet be . . .

Harper hurled the container into the decomp and fled back to her quarters.

Maybe Drake drank that so-called tomato juice, then indulged her erotic wants with Harper, thus satisfying both hungers separately but fully. Or perhaps she had simply used her sexual magnetism with cold calculation — to dull Harper's perceptions and suspicions. That would be why Drake had been the tireless aggressor in their lovemaking, and Harper its pleasure-blind recipient. Or perhaps Drake was waiting for this time when they were in the asteroid belt and cut off from all communication, perhaps this was when she would make love for the final time and in its aftermath dine lavishly on the freshly flowing blood of one supine, blissfully comatose Lieutenant T. M. Harper . . .

Harper leaped to her feet and resealed her door, setting in a new privacy code. Then she sat down heavily on her bed.

There was no escape. Drake would simply run computer sequences until the correct portal-opening code came up. And even if the ship's communications system was at this moment operative, what could be more ludicrous than to transmit to Headquarters a message that she was trapped in outer space with a vampire? And after they had finished laughing, after Drake had finished laughing as well, Drake would take her final satisfactions, then dump Harper's drained corpse out a hatch and report her lost in space, a victim of suicide. And heaven knew Headquarters would believe it — insanity and suicide had never been uncommon in the Service despite the psych probes . . .

Harper glanced at her chronometer. It was almost nineteen hundred hours, Drake's usual time to appear. In so depleted a state she surely would not be leaving her quarters tonight — not until she had recovered sufficiently to guide *Scorpio IV* from the asteroid belt.

From her bedside console Harper again called up the ship's library. Again she consulted *Vampires, characteristics,* and studied the text for some time. With a sigh she turned off the fax and lay back, hands behind her head.

Certainly there were ways to defend herself. She merely needed to plunge a wooden stake into Drake's heart, or cut off her head. Unfortunately, spacecraft were not equipped with wooden stakes or implements with which to dispatch someone's head. Drake would also have a very serious problem if Harper could figure out a way to find and destroy her coffin. Or there was the Trad religious rite — stalking a quailing Drake with a cross clutched in her hand until Drake leaped out a hatch, grateful to escape so horrifying an object. Or she could perhaps keep Drake at bay by wearing a necklace of garlic cloves — except that compatibility rules had placed garlic on the restricted list of allowable spacecraft edibles.

Harper had long since given vent to laughter which turned into wild hysteria.

She had to be crazy. Or was she crazy? She had to know. Because she had to do something.

* * * * *

Knowing she could not sleep, unable to bear the confinement of her quarters, Harper went up to the observation deck. She again called up the ship's library and the subject haunting her thoughts. After a time she began to pace.

"Good evening, Harper."

Whirling, she stared incredulously. She had to be hallucinating. The gaunt, desperately weak Drake of only four hours ago had vanished, to be replaced by the Drake of before, clad in her usual black pants and an emerald shirt — a beautiful, vital, regal Drake with all of her strength and magnetism restored.

Drake carried a container of tomato juice. She sipped from it, and then said quietly, "Once my work is finished I need only a few hours of rest. My recuperative powers are quite strong."

Her eyes fixing on the drink in Drake's hand, Harper thought: *Or is the real truth that it's nighttime now, and the night is your time . . .*

"Minimal work needs to be accomplished," Drake continued, "and we will be ready for departure."

That slightly accented voice . . . Drake is European, she's from a village near Bucharest . . .

"Are you well?" inquired Drake, her dark eyes narrowing.

"Am I well," Harper repeated. She watched Drake walk to her chaise, the strides easy and graceful.

Either I'm crazy or I'm not. And either way, at this point I have nothing to lose . . .

She took a deep breath. "Are you familiar with the name Bram Stoker?"

Drake did not change expression. "A nineteenth century historian."

"A nineteenth century novelist," Harper corrected her. "Author of a novel popular well into the twenty-first century."

"A historian," Drake countered with cool emphasis. "And a most limited one at that. He recorded in fictional form what glimmerings he knew of an entire species." She added, "I possess extensive knowledge in this area."

"Yes." Harper gestured to the lighted fax and then clasped her hands tightly together to prevent them from shaking. "I found thousands of references in the ship's library."

Drake studied Harper, her eyes an opaque darkness.

Harper thought of an enduring nineteenth century short story in which a man chose one of two fateful doors. In this situation it was not a matter of the lady or the tiger; it could only be both . . .

"I have come to believe," Harper said, her voice soft with the desperate truth of her words, "that either you are a . . . a member of that species Bram Stoker wrote about, or I am insane."

"I see." Drake's voice was mild. "On what do you base your . . . belief?"

"A lot of small things," Harper whispered. "Things about your behavior, and this ship. But mostly . . . " She closed her eyes for a moment. "I saw you — or I think I saw you — turn into a . . . bat."

Under Drake's narrowed, piercing gaze, Harper sank onto the sofa, her legs unwilling to support her.

Then Drake said, "Basic self-protection would dictate that I agree with your suggestion of insanity. But I cannot allow you to believe you have gone mad."

Able only slowly to absorb the stunning implication of Drake's words, Harper looked away from the pale face and the intense eyes. She tried to speak and failed, tried again: "How can you possibly be a . . . a . . . "

"Vampire," Drake supplied.

Harper focused on the emerald color of Drake's shirt, a jewel-like vividness against the surreal blue-white crystalline swirl in the view windows. She said, almost pleadingly, "I *must* be crazy. How can you be a starship captain and a . . . vampire?"

"I was born with considerable innate intelligence which I have sometimes been able to make use of during the eight hundred and twenty-two years of my existence."

She felt as if her mind had been set adrift, away from any mooring to coherent thought. "Uh, you mean you were born in the year . . . in . . . " Her mathematic acuity had deserted her.

"Seventeen sixty-seven," Drake said. "More than a century before Bram Stoker wrote *Dracula*."

"How . . . how could . . . "

"How did I become as I am?"

Stricken mute, Harper nodded.

Drake shifted her gaze to the fax. Her face hardened. "Stoker painted his dark brush over all of my species, but no writer of either truth or fiction could possibly portray the vileness of the creature . . . "

She looked again at Harper. "In my village I lived with my husband and his niece. I was twenty-seven then. My husband was an old man, and infirm. His niece and I were lovers. It was an arrangement quite common in those times.

"Late one night Nadja and I were in the garden. Had we not been so deeply in embrace we would have heard and escaped our intruder. He bludgeoned me unconscious." The voice was expressionless. "He took the blood from Nadja right there in our garden. I later learned that she perished under his blows beforehand, and thus escaped the vampire contagion — she rests peacefully and forevermore in her grave.

"Me he carried away with him. He had bound me, and the next night, when he rose from his earthen place, he satisfied his wants in a loathsome fashion quite beyond all your imagining."

Harper, her eyes riveted on Drake, was unable to speak had she wanted to.

"He left me bound still, and barely living. The following night he came to me again and this time his appetites rendered me lifeless. But of course I later rose from the earthen mound beside him — a creature like him. He expected that I would welcome his bestowal of another existence after death. And like most men, particularly of that time, he had presumed that regardless of my screams or my struggle, in actuality I had welcomed his ravages."

Drake drew a leg up, clasped a hand over a knee. "It was only a matter of careful planning before I was able, early one morning, to drive a stake through him. I did so quite slowly — he was bound securely enough to nullify his great strength, and was as helpless to me as I had been for him. Then I dragged his disgusting remains outside to await the cleansing rays of the sun."

For some time there was silence; Drake appeared immersed in this particular memory. Then she said, "During those times existence of my species was at its most difficult. Vampire hordes lay nighttime siege to entire villages. And those villagers foolish enough to venture from their locked homes, or to give unwitting admittance to my kind, met a grisly fate that added yet more undead to our ranks. The church denied our existence as the heretical superstition of ignorant peasants, and government officials, obedient to the church, refused to send soldiers. In daytime the desperate villagers marauded the entire countryside seeking us, destroying us where we slept. At night they came out in mobs, with torches and axes and stakes, to encounter us directly — in defiance of our nighttime powers. They took terrible casualties in those battles, but they further thinned our ranks. I maintained my own existence by taking my needs from among the villagers newly dead."

She paused to study Harper. "You do not shudder at such details."

Harper, who had been shuddering internally, said with difficulty, "It seems an agonizing . . . It seems you . . . lived as you could."

Drake's faint smile instantly faded. "Always I have existed as I could. After the battles were over and the vampire hordes destroyed, I left the cave where I had concealed myself during the daylight hours. I possessed sufficient androgyny to conceal my true sex, and in those days it was essential that I do so in order to travel safely. And I soon learned to endure the excruciating pain of transforming my human body to mammalian form when necessary. It had become quite clear to me how I must live if I wished to maintain my existence."

She gazed at a point somewhere over Harper's shoulder. "I became a presence on virtually every field where men clashed in battle. There was no war whose inhuman suffering I did not witness."

In dawning understanding Harper whispered, "You mean from the eighteenth century you — "

"I witnessed carnage beyond your worst nightmares, on the soils of every land. I was present in America during the grossly inhuman slaughter of your Civil War, I was with American soldiers in all your foreign wars. I was at Verdun, Dunkirk, Hiroshima, Kuwait, Moscow . . . There was not a moment during those centuries when I could not find sustenance from the newly dead on some nation's battlefields."

Harper asked numbly, "You were never discovered? Suspected?"

"I was cloaked always by darkness. And for the dead in battle, no examination is ever made of them except for the obvious death-dealing wounds."

Harper uttered, "Were there . . . others of you?"

"Yes. There was vast provender, more than enough for us all."

Harper closed her eyes. "Then how many of you . . . are there?"

"I have no way of knowing." Drake shrugged. "For very good reasons I believe that only the fittest of us ever continue to survive. And we have learned there is safety in numbers — small numbers. We have also learned to be exceedingly clever at concealment — so much so that we are mostly invisible to one another as well."

Harper stared at her. "All those years, those decades, all these centuries . . . you've spent them . . . alone?"

"Not always." Drake sighed. "I met women, yes. Some I grew very close to. Some I believe loved me." She seemed to reflect over, to choose her words. "For endless years I touched none of them, allowed none to touch me. Having never forgotten the sight of others like me in their frenzied feeding upon the living, I dared not trust what the touch of living flesh might cause in me."

Harper inhaled slowly. What had the touch of her own living flesh caused in Drake?

"Then I returned to my country. I had not come back since . . . " After a moment Drake continued, "But in the year twenty twenty-one I had to return. And as you know, I returned as mourner."

Harper nodded somberly at Drake's allusion to the "limited" East-West engagement waged over the hapless, innocent buffer countries of Eastern Europe, a soul-searing catastrophe which had begun to heal only a century or so ago.

"With the borders sealed, I entered from the Black Sea as a medical volunteer. Hundreds of millions were dead, but tens of thousands were still living, awaiting death from the irreversible chemicals in their bodies . . .

"It was in my village that I met Eva. She was but twenty-three years old, and the virulence lay gathering within her — but she was filled with the vibrant life, the innocence, the hopefulness of a child. She was to me a mirror image of my dearest Nadja, and amid all that devastation our love grew like a miraculous flower . . .

"The vampire legends had lingered in the villages of my country. Eva had grown up with them. Her clear, unsophisticated insight penetrated my defenses . . . she instinctively knew what I was. She came to me for love and would not hear of my fears, would not countenance danger. Afterward, when her illness struck, I gave her what strength I could to cushion her terrible, bewildered grief over her mortality, and when the time came I eased her path into death, having already given in to her wish for the vampire kiss, for life afterward with me."

The vampire kiss . . . Involuntarily, Harper placed a hand over her heart.

Drake looked down at her own hands, turned them over, examined them. "It is as I told you, Harper — for my species it is survival of only the very fittest. Eva could not bear the way we had to exist. Our wholly nocturnal lives, the secrecy, the hiding, the constant movement to protect ourselves, our need of that very specific sustenance, the entire dark nether world of our lives. Once, she was shut away by the authorities in Chile — she had been found wandering at night in a state of mental collapse. It was very difficult for me to obtain her release before she perished under their unwitting hands. But it was soon after that that one morning she walked out into the sunlight. I know she wished to protect me from her increasingly dangerous fragility, but I believe she had also come to need the peace of death far more than my love. We had been together nine years."

"I'm sorry," Harper murmured, "I'm truly sorry."

Drake nodded acknowledgement. "Her death drastically weakened my own emotional structure. Eventually I resumed my nomadic and solitary life, and thereafter, when I met a woman who found me desirable, I gave her nothing. Nothing. Finally she would drift away as I knew she would, leaving me again to myself."

Harper was pierced by the poignance of these revelations which served also to explain Drake's behavior with her. Never would she trade one year of her natural span for any number of years of Drake's half-life . . . She murmured, "I consider myself a loner, but I couldn't bear such loneliness as yours."

Drake gave her a smile of melancholy warmth. "I judge you to be independent-minded and courageous. One day an individual will love and respect that strength . . . You're very young, Harper, with a fierce grip on life. Tenacity kept me living too — at first. But during those terrible early years, I was certain I would simply walk into the sunlight one morning and put an end to it.

"Then I discovered something outside myself and virtually unknown to a woman born of my time: art. And with that art came maturation of my intellect. At various times throughout the centuries I have been a musician, philosopher, historian, sculptor, writer, artist — disappearing and changing my profession when too much fame or public scrutiny forced me to do so. And then late in the twenty-first century I discovered the challenges of advanced space-age technology . . . " Drake trailed off, lost in reflection.

Harper shook her throbbing head. The thesis that she was sane seemed to be again unraveling. She needed to know about that vampire kiss, she needed other answers as well. She asked, "Back then, was that when you laid the groundwork for becoming a starship captain?"

"It had its genesis then, yes."

Again Harper shook her head. "I can't imagine how you've accomplished any of this." She gestured with both hands to take in the spacecraft. "You're contracted to ExxTel, everyone knows about the thoroughness of their information network. I can't see how anyone could possibly slip through such a sieve."

Drake smiled. "What if I told you I have access to my records, that I can input and erase whatever data I choose?"

"I wouldn't believe you," Harper said flatly. Drake's suggestion was preposterous. "They have a standing offer of a billion credits to anyone who can break through their maze of protective programs."

"What use do I have for a billion credits? Self-protection is my single concern. Their systems were indeed interesting and ingenious — they required sixty-five years to penetrate." Drake shrugged at the gaping Harper. "I had more than enough time to devote to the challenge of the puzzle."

It was all too incredible. Too many incredible facts piling one onto the other. She was crazy, Drake was crazy, it was all crazy. Harper said sardonically, "I suppose that's how you rose to become a starship captain — falsifying records?"

"In small part. I obtained education and specific training in unconventional ways, but I advanced along traditional career paths. An enduring human instinct is to avoid nocturnal hours — and so ample opportunities exist for those willing to live and work in the darkness. Periodically I enter ExxTel's files to adjust my name and date of birth and other facts relating to me. In a monolith such as ExxTel, the personnel I interface with come and go, leaving insufficient continuity to bring suspicion."

Harper felt an icy touch of fear. "Am I the only one then who . . . knows about this?"

Drake studied her. "Over time, few have even remotely suspected. Since the twentieth century my greatest protection has been the refusal to believe vampire legends — especially by scientifically grounded persons such as yourself. To my knowledge, none of the women accompanying me to the

Antares asteroid belt have ever added together the clues I cannot help but provide."

And it was by purest accident, Harper admitted ruefully, that she herself had. "There haven't been any men on your voyages?"

"I request only female military liaisons, and the Space Service has always acceded."

Harper blurted, "I suppose you've made love to them as you did with me."

"Yes," Drake said.

Harper forced her stunned mind into motion. If all this was actually true, then those other women who had accompanied Drake . . . surely she could not have managed to infect them all? Yes, she answered herself, she could have. And if she had, none of them might ever realize it until their deaths decades from now, when they tried to rise from under the straps binding them onto a conveyor feeding them into a crematorium . . .

"What have you done to me?" she choked. She was hurtling down a corridor of terror. "If you're really a vampire, you satisfy your sexuality only in the act of feeding. What have you *done* to me?"

"I have enjoyed you fully."

The hair rose on the back of Harper's neck; she rubbed a frenzied hand across it. "In the name of anything sacred," she hissed, "how did you give me your vampire kiss?"

"I have not given it to you, nor to anyone since Eva."

Harper exhaled, her limbs suddenly trembling.

"When my dying Eva wanted me to make love to her, I could not refuse. And I discovered with her the greatest ecstasy of my life. Greater even than with Nadja. Because I learned that another kind of fluid can also nourish me. It too is a vital fluid — from that place in a woman that creates life. You give it generously. You give it during that length of time when I am most fully enjoying you, and even more copiously as you approach and then experience the heights of orgasm."

Looking seriously at Harper, Drake added, "You're turning quite red."

"My Trad upbringing," Harper muttered, rubbing at her flaming face.

Drake continued, "I made love to you only because you wanted me. I come only to a woman who wants me."

Harper shook her head in bafflement. Certainly she had not invited that first approach from Drake . . .

"I have the capability of assuming mammal form. As a consequence I also have a highly developed olfactory sense. I knew of your desire and arousal, I could smell that nourishment I so keenly enjoy."

Again Harper felt her face flame. Mortified, feeling stripped of every defense, she lashed out, "How could you take such advantage of me? And all those other women? Don't you feel any *responsibility?*"

"Harper, have you not enjoyed what we shared together? How have I taken advantage?"

"You preyed on me. Preyed on all of us. Played with our emotions. You — "

"Harper." Drake pushed a lock of hair from her forehead, then sat up on her chaise and circled her arms around her knees. "Harper, have you at any time felt love for me?"

Harper looked at her. At the creamy smoothness of the pale face, the finely chiseled, aristocratic features, the elegant slenderness. Furious at feeling within her the edges of desire, she hurled the unvarnished, tactless truth: "No."

Drake nodded and smiled, as if Harper were a bright pupil who had found the only logical response to an illogical question. "I've given you nothing to love. Not for decades have I given anything that anyone could love."

"You think that confers some kind of nobility? You
wanted me, you've made love to me every single night. Didn't
you care anything about me at all?"

Her face closing, Drake did not respond.

It occurred to Harper that while Drake had given nothing
of herself, she had opened her own self to Drake in every way.
She said carefully, "Have you become attached to any of your
women companions during your months alone with them in
space?"

Drake looked away from her.

"Please. I need you to tell me."

Drake said tonelessly, "You've been a captivating and
admirable companion, my physical gratifications have been
extraordinary, this has been in all ways the loveliest of voyages.
I have given as much physical pleasure as I know how to give, I
have taken in return the by-product of your pleasure. Beyond
that, since there is no future for us, there is nothing more to be
said." She turned resolutely away from Harper.

Studying the poetic handsomeness of Drake's face in
profile, she absorbed this response. Her glance fell on the
drink Drake had placed on the module beside her. "Tell me,"
she said, deflecting the topic still vibrating between them,
"when you don't have a woman to make love to, where do you
get the blood you need?"

Drake turned quickly back to her. "I use existing
technology to synthesize it." She seemed relieved at the new
direction of Harper's questions. "But synthetic blood is
not . . . " She searched for a term, then said with an amiable
shrug, "It is lacking. For you it would be as if you were always
surrounded by appetizing food yet limited to consuming only
gruel. But it does sustain me, and in a manner which is ethically
necessary."

Harper pointed to the tomato juice. "Is that what
you . . . consume?"

"No." Drake smiled. "I like its smell, which seems earthy and warm, and the color, which is . . . " She trailed off.

"How often must you take your nourishment?"

"It's variable. I can and do frequently exist in a famished state for weeks. After I have truly feasted, as I have during this time with you, then I prefer to exist without food for a lengthy time afterward rather than return to . . . my gruel."

"You mean you diet between women." She could not account for her sense of betrayal, her jealousy and resentment. "For those few weeks until another woman comes on board."

Drake did not respond.

Harper's ire turned against itself. Why belabor this woman, whose singular and determined morality had redefined the compelling needs of her nature? Harper said, "And you've never told any other women on these voyages anything about this."

"Only you. Since you are the only one who has ever guessed."

Harper voiced a new apprehension: "Why tell me? Aren't you afraid I'll expose you, tear down this whole facade?"

Drake fixed weary eyes on her. "I become ever more bored with the facade. I become less and less patient with the restrictions of my existence."

Harper nodded. In Drake's place her own patience would have exhausted itself centuries ago. She said, "I saw your quarters, the blackness. Do you actually keep a coffin in there?"

Drake chuckled. "That part of the legend is somewhat exaggerated. We do need darkness during the hours of the sun, and complete darkness is most beneficial. The smallness of my quarters, this tiny ship in the vastness of space — it's equivalent enough to a coffin. In my quarters I have collected soil from many places on Earth, especially my own land, and I sleep with it gathered around me. It seems to bring me peace."

Drake smiled at her. "For your own sake I must solemnly caution you against attempting to reveal me. You are indeed sane, but others will probably not agree."

"True," Harper said, grinning at the thought of relating these astounding events to anyone — especially when she herself was convinced only intermittently that she was not hallucinating.

"In any case I am never truly safe," Drake mused. "I know that if I continue to live, one day they will come for me. With their stakes and axes, just as they came so many centuries ago in my village. Human beings always believe their own era to be more enlightened than any before, but they still avoid examination of the origin of their own food, their own blood-drenched sustenance. And of all taboos, cannibalism remains the ultimate perversion. Even those who are not affected by xenophobia would hesitate to extend tolerance to a vampire."

She gazed out at the whirling crystals. "Eva learned that immortality does not bring with it the will or the desire to live. For centuries I have held and kept the power of life. But Harper, more and more I dream about dying. I dream about journeying to a particularly gracious star system — perhaps the Pleiades — and allowing my ship to simply fall into one of its lovely stars. But mostly I dream of returning to Earth."

Drake looked at her; Harper was held unmoving by the grieving dark eyes. "I dream of the sun, Harper. I long for it. I often wonder if, when I walk out into that sun, I will know for an instant its warmth as I remember it, as I used to know it . . . before it begins the disintegration of my flesh . . . "

"You have too much to offer . . . " Harper faltered; there were no words to comfort the immense tragedy of Drake's existence. "You have . . . priceless gifts for the ages to come."

"Yes." Drake's voice held an ironic edge. "When our voyage is over, Harper, you will walk away forever and forget. There is no choice."

"Walk away, I must," Harper said slowly. "But forget you, never."

Drake's smile bathed her in its tenderness. "That is the one immortality all of us hope for."

Harper gazed wistfully back at her. "If only I had learned about you sooner. I have two months — only two months — to hear eight centuries of eyewitness Earth history."

"Yes," Drake said, her voice suddenly eager.

Drake's beauty seemed to have acquired a youthful energy and sheen, and Harper looked at her in affection. "I still need to adjust to what you've told me," she said with a grin, "especially about my body being food for you."

"Your body is not my food," Drake gently corrected her. "Your pleasure is my food."

"I know I don't taste like gruel," Harper said, still smiling. "Do I taste like some other specific food?"

"The pleasures of you are infinitely lovely," Drake said softly. "Each night, and throughout the lovemaking of each night, there are differences, you taste differently everywhere. Your mouth is sometimes like sweet spring water, sometimes like cream. Your body varies everywhere in taste and smell, the scents are like grass and rain, sometimes like peaches or apples or berries. Your breasts taste like buttered honey, your thighs contain the most intoxicating spice . . . " She trailed off, looking closely at Harper.

Feeling the heat in her body rise to her face, knowing she had no defense whatever, Harper said recklessly, "And the place you've left out?"

Drake rose from her chaise, came to her. "Sweet wine that slowly intensifies into flavors I will not attempt to describe."

Taking Drake's hands, Harper murmured, "Is it possible . . . to return the ship to weightlessness?"

"Of course. Every night, all the way back. But later," she whispered, reaching for Harper. "At this moment I smell sweet wine . . . "

* * * * *

Harper walked down the ramp directly into the debrief section of Moon Station 13. She did not look back.

Sergeant Stewart saluted smartly, then commandeered her gear bubble. "Welcome back, Lieutenant." A Briton, he pronounced her ranking as Leftenant. "You look splendid. Had a bit of trouble up there, we heard."

She looked at him sharply.

"The deflection shield," he said, his thin face creasing in puzzlement.

"Oh, that," she said casually, covering her alarm. "A momentary problem for Captain Drake."

"Remarkable work, that. Can't say I know much about her, nobody ever says much. How were the four months with her?"

Harper turned then, and looked back at *Scorpio IV* where the robodrones were already assembling to unload the crystals. It was seven hundred hours, and Drake, she knew, would be in her quarters, those quarters that were as black as the grave . . .

"Routine," Harper answered the Sergeant. "The mission was routine."

He shrugged. "The onboard data seems fairly clearcut. Debrief shouldn't take more than half an hour, I would think."

Alone in her quarters afterward, she deposited her gear bubble. She scanned messages from Niklaus and several acquaintances she'd made here on Moon Station 13. The final message contained a privacy seal. Curious, she entered her ID code and pressed the palms of both hands on the ID reader.

The striking dark-eyed woman looking back at her wore her black hair cropped short, sheaves of it like petals around her face and down over her forehead. Several mission ribbons hung under the Lieutenant's silver bar on her Space Service jacket.

"Welcome back, Lieutenant Harper. My name's Westra, of the Science Corps. I saw the alert come over the base intercom

about your shield trouble. When I found out who your captain was, I knew you'd both make it back just fine.

The woman on the screen smiled. *"I was with Captain Drake two years ago on a similar mission to Antares. She advised me then that she could not form emotional attachments to her military passengers, and would not grant me permission to visit her should our paths again intersect — a decision I have no choice but to accept."*

Rapt, Harper stared as the woman on the screen smiled again, a slow, private smile.

"From the repros I've seen of you, you appear to be someone I would find . . . interesting. If I appear the same way to you, then perhaps we could meet and share a beverage together . . . and also share some of our memories of Captain Drake . . . "

The message ended with the printout of a telecode number.

Bemused, Harper played the message back. Then played it back once more, this time without the sound, freezing the frame when that slow, private smile began.

Lieutenant Westra did indeed look interesting, Harper decided. That dark hair, those intelligent dark eyes, that perfectly lovely looking mouth . . . Smiling, Harper reflected that along with her discovery of the pleasures to be had with a woman, she had also learned that she definitely preferred a dark woman . . .

What would it be like, she wondered, to share pleasure fully with a woman, to explore and experience what Drake had enjoyed in her?

Staring at the seductively smiling figure on the screen, she absently erased the other messages, including the one from Niklaus. Then she opened her private comm channel and entered the telecode for Lieutenant Westra.

THE TEST

Steepling her fingers, Dr. Newell studied the Petersons. "Richard and Mary," she said gently, "your daughter will suffer the gravest kind of trauma unless you have *highly* substantive reasons for believing she is a lesbian." Her light blue eyes shifted to the folder on her desk. "There is no genetic confirmation whatever."

Richard said anxiously, "We realize she doesn't have the gene, but she — "

"It's not a gene. The discovery involves a specific genetic configuration, a *signature*." The doctor spoke with weary patience, as if she had explained this distinction countless times before.

"Yes. Well . . . " Fingering his tie, Richard adjusted his shoulders in his navy blue suit jacket. "We knew from the day she was born she didn't have it, and of course Mary and I don't either. It comes out in how she is and the way she *acts*, you see. From what we hear, that's enough to test her for a recessive . . . whatever you people want to call it."

"A recessive genetic signature." The white-coated psychologist sighed. "A great many other parents are making similar decisions about their children — and are inflicting severe psychological damage." Studying the grim, set faces, Dr. Newell added with resignation, "Describe specifically how she acts."

"Like a complete tomboy," Mary answered sharply. "She *insists* on being called Casey. And she's very different from her peer group, doctor." Her voice had softened into more deferential tones. "The only playmates she'll have are other girls, and they're different, too. None of them tend to act in the traditional ways of — "

"Normalcy. Heterosexuality," Richard finished dourly.

Dr. Newell's gaze narrowed on Mary; she took in the carefully coiffed brown-blonde hair, the smartly styled plum-colored dress, the high-heeled sandals. "Mary," she said softly, "Cassandra is only nine years old. That's typically a tomboy age. And her behavior may be a reaction to . . . " She spoke meaningfully to both Petersons, " . . . outside pressures."

"We think differently," Mary said through tight lips.

The doctor tapped a few keys on the computer access near her elbow. "So she's formed primary female relationships within her peer group." Her low-toned voice clearly conveyed skepticism. "What other specific behavior patterns?" Her fingers remained poised over the keys.

Richard said with more than a touch of belligerence, "She likes the out-of-doors. Likes nothing more than to hike and camp. Her girl friends are the same way — "

"These days more and more of them seem to be," the doctor observed darkly.

"You've seen her, doctor, you'll have to admit she's unusually well-muscled — "

"Everything you're saying is a thoroughly discredited stereotype." The doctor's tone was not harsh. She continued to tap more keys. "Some of the most delicate, non-athletic women you can imagine are lesbians. Some of — "

"We know all that," Mary interrupted, her tone once again sharp with insistence. "We're telling you it's a whole combination of things. She's a leader-type, assertive — bold as you please about taking charge of everything."

"More promising," the doctor conceded, "but not necessarily indicative either." She abandoned the computer keys and placed both hands on the desk, one over the other. The hands were strong, capable-looking. "I realize she's very young. But has she exhibited any concrete evidence of sexual identity?"

"She's very attached to her playmates," Mary said primly. "Very attached."

The doctor clenched her hands and closed her eyes briefly. "Again, that's normal at her age. You said she had only female playmates. It's understandable she'd form — "

"There are boys her age at school." Richard's broad shoulders were hunched with tension. "Her grades are better than theirs. The teachers say she's precocious."

"With the condition your schools have fallen into, that's no — "

"Look." The word snapped whip-like in the room. Mary glared at the psychologist. "You're supposed to help us. That's your *job*. To seek out any children who might be homosexual because of this recessive — "

"Listen to me." Doctor Newell's raised voice commanded silence. "It's a vital part of my job to prevent children from undergoing a traumatic and unnecessary ordeal because overzealous parents suspect a recessive genetic pattern which is so rare as to be — "

"But it *is* possible and we have to *know*." Mary bit off the words. "She's nine years old. If it does turn out she actually is a lesbian, then you people can *help* her . . . "

"Richard and Mary, I ask you one last time — *please* reconsider. Can you not simply accept Cassandra as she is?"

The Petersons looked at each other. Mary took Richard's hand. "No," Richard said. The couple shook their heads in added emphasis.

"It's an entire battery of tests," the psychologist said tiredly. "Cognitive, attitudinal, reactive — "

"We want the answer once and for all," Mary said. "We want Casey tested."

Dr. Newell's sigh was audible. She touched a key on the computer; a consent form flicked out of a slot on the desk. She picked it up, drew a pen from her tunic top and made an X, then slid the form across the desk top. "Sign here."

The Petersons made their way into a large waiting area divided into separate enclaves, each enclave furnished with bright red chairs and sofas and tables against glowing white walls and white carpeting. Dozens of other parents were already waiting, some pacing the area's perimeter or sitting in those sections equipped with television; others read magazines or simply stared into space. The area was hushed; none of the parents communicated with anyone else.

Concealed behind an opaque screen, a white-clad, dark-haired young man sat at a desk overseeing the entire scene. Several times before it had been his assignment to be here, and he well understood the silence, the resistance to communication among the parents: they felt themselves to be in a dread competition, and could bear only anonymous contact with other parents whose child might pass while their own might fail.

The young man, immersed in assembling data for his own survey work, occasionally answered a question from a parent who pressed a query button under one of the communication screens. The questions were usually routine, and always whispered:

It's been two hours. Do you give out interim test results?

No, he transmitted in electronic response.

How many children have tested positive so far today?

Information released on a monthly basis only, he replied.

His answers were always terse, aloof. He could do nothing to relieve their anxiety, and he remained an invisible, voiceless presence because the slightest indication of friendliness or concern would bring all of the parents flocking to receive a similar perceived benediction — as if to cast some subtle good fortune on their own particular offspring.

The Petersons sat on one of the sofas for half an hour, then got up and joined those parents pacing an endless circle around the perimeter. After a time the Petersons left the trek and walked outside to gaze silently at the manicured landscape, then up at the emerald walls of the Center for the Advancement of Humankind, its tower vanishing into the bright blue sky. Even though they had been told that testing of their daughter would consume a full four hours, they soon went back inside to pace, and to wait.

The parents, one group after another, were summoned by a signal on the ID insignia each wore. They would be given the test results privately, along with appropriate counseling recommendations, then pick up their child and leave by another exit.

The Petersons were among the last parents to be called.

* * * * *

Dr. Newell awaited them in a cubicle furnished with a desk and two metal chairs. Expressionless, she gestured for the Petersons to be seated. They obeyed, Mary smoothing her hands repeatedly over the skirt of her dress, Richard hunching his shoulders.

Dr. Newell said evenly, "Your daughter's test result is negative."

The Petersons sagged in their chairs.

"You have considerable damage to repair." The doctor's voice was quiet, firm. "Because of your contention of abnormality in your daughter, you've given her every reason to believe she's failed you." She pushed a form toward them. "Take this, these are your instructions. You've committed yourselves to treatment for her. It's vital that you follow through."

Richard nodded, his blue eyes tearing. He folded the paper, slid it into his inside breast pocket.

"I can't believe this," Mary said, her face ashen. "I'm sure there's some mistake, I'm sure another test — "

"Mary, you know the rules. The test is fully validated, the result is incontestible. We're just as anxious as you to identify special children, but we don't practice child abuse." There was a slight emphasis on the "we."

"It looked like there was something," Richard whispered. "We were positive we saw something."

"You tried to pervert this child into ways unnatural to her because of your own wishful thinking," the psychologist pronounced quietly.

Mary's eyes were closed. "You can't blame us. If she'd passed, you'd put her in the finest of schools, her whole future would — "

"Richard and Mary, you have a lovely, perfectly normal heterosexual child. Accept her as she is." She touched a button on her desk top. "Take Cassandra home and love her."

A side door opened. A brown-haired young girl wearing jeans and a red shirt sidled into the room, her face blotchy, her hazel eyes red-rimmed. "Mom, Dad, I'm sorry," she blubbered.

"It's all right," her mother said, managing a smile. "It's all right, Cassandra."

Richard said, "This is our fault, honey, not yours."

The parents embraced their daughter. Arms around one another, the Peterson family walked slowly from the room, down a corridor toward the exit. The psychologist, her fingers steepled, watched with a compassion that deepened to pity.

The young man who had been overseeing the waiting area entered the room; he carried his survey report. "That's the last of the parents for today."

He looked more closely at the doctor. "My friend, you look drained. Why don't you and Ginny bring the family over tonight for a relaxing dinner with Adam and me?"

She smiled, some of her exhaustion easing at the thought of her lover and their children. "It sounds wonderful, Steve."

"Another washout day?"

The psychologist nodded, the tiredness settling in once again. "You know the odds as well as I do. I wish we had some option other than to offer this charity, this pathetic exercise."

The young man tapped his survey report on the desk. "There's revised information, Eve. Life-expectancy among the normals has fallen another nine percent. Their birth rate since the discovery is down sixty-eight point five percent. And both curves are in accelerated decline."

"Yes," she said simply.

"I know we predicted something like this. But so soon?"

"I'm not in the least surprised." Dr. Newell made one final computer entry, signed off, turned to the young man. "Imagine knowing beyond a shadow of a doubt that all those individuals in your species with exceptional intelligence or creativity possess a precise genetic configuration, either dominant or recessive — and that you don't. Imagine learning that throughout history the genetic configuration has been passed from individuals who were invariably homosexual, either latent or overt. Imagine realizing that you and all those like you are now obsolete, are useless biological fodder."

The young man nodded. "It all seems to correlate to that other clearly dominant species on earth — the dinosaurs. I'm beginning to believe what's happening to the normals is the reason why the most spectacular animal fauna in history suddenly vanished."

"I'm convinced of it. We have good evidence that members of a species share subconscious awareness with other members of that species. It's reasonable to assume that when evolution left the dinosaurs fatally flawed and obsolete, instinctual awareness caused a once-dominant species to lose its will to live — to immediately stop reproducing. Today, those few normals who have a child do everything from the moment of its birth to force it into homosexuality, to prove the existence of a recessive genetic signature in both the child and themselves. But once the child fails the test . . . The parents never bring the child back for counseling, they produce no more children. They're dinosaurs and they concede it."

"I feel sorry for them." Circling the psychologist's shoulders with an arm, the young man walked with her from the room.

"But all our own brothers and sisters before us," he said softly, "they haunt me, Eve. They held on to what they truly were and paid so dearly for it . . . If only they could have understood why so many people feared and persecuted us, why the churches fought us, fought everything connected with reproductive freedom, fought the whole concept of evolution — why they hated us with such instinctive desperation."

"Instinctive desperation is right," said Eve Newell quietly, tightening her arm around the young man. "From biblical times, from the very dawning of our species, racial foreknowledge told the normals that we represented humankind's next step on the ladder of evolution — that the homosexual is homo superior."

Together, an arm around each other, they left the Centre for the Advancement of Humankind.

A few of the publications of
THE NAIAD PRESS, INC.
P.O. Box 10543 • Tallahassee, Florida 32302
Phone (904) 539-9322
Mail orders welcome. Please include 15% postage.

DREAMS AND SWORDS by Katherine V. Forrest. 192 pp. Romantic, erotic, imaginative stories. ISBN 0-941483-03-7 $8.95

MEMORY BOARD by Jane Rule. 336 pp. Memorable novel about an aging lesbian couple. ISBN 0-941483-02-9 8.95

THE ALWAYS ANONYMOUS BEAST by Lauren Wright Douglas. 224 pp. A Caitlin Reece mystery. First in a series.
ISBN 0-941483-04-5 8.95

SEARCHING FOR SPRING by Patricia A. Murphy. 224 pp. Novel about the recovery of love. ISBN 0-941483-00-2 8.95

DUSTY'S QUEEN OF HEARTS DINER by Lee Lynch. 240 pp. Romantic blue-collar novel. ISBN 0-941483-01-0 8.95

PARENTS MATTER by Ann Muller. 240 pp. Parents' relationships with lesbian daughters and gay sons.
ISBN 0-930044-91-6 9.95

THE PEARLS by Shelley Smith. 176 pp. Passion and fun in the Caribbean sun. ISBN 0-930044-93-2 7.95

MAGDALENA by Sarah Aldridge. 352 pp. Epic Lesbian novel set on three continents. ISBN 0-930044-99-1 8.95

THE BLACK AND WHITE OF IT by Ann Allen Shockley. 144 pp. Short stories. ISBN 0-930044-96-7 $7.95

SAY JESUS AND COME TO ME by Ann Allen Shockley. 288 pp. Contemporary romance. ISBN 0-930044-98-3 8.95

LOVING HER by Ann Allen Shockley. 192 pp. Romantic love story. ISBN 0-930044-97-5 7.95

MURDER AT THE NIGHTWOOD BAR by Katherine V. Forrest. 240 pp. A Kate Delafield mystery. Second in a series.
ISBN 0-930044-92-4 8.95

ZOE'S BOOK by Gail Pass. 224 pp. Passionate, obsessive love story. ISBN 0-930044-95-9 7.95

WINGED DANCER by Camarin Grae. 228 pp. Erotic Lesbian adventure story. ISBN 0-930044-88-6 8.95

PAZ by Camarin Grae. 336 pp. Romantic Lesbian adventurer with the power to change the world. ISBN 0-930044-89-4 8.95

SOUL SNATCHER by Camarin Grae. 224 pp. A puzzle, an adventure, a mystery—Lesbian romance.
ISBN 0-930044-90-8 8.95

THE LOVE OF GOOD WOMEN by Isabel Miller. 224 pp. Long-awaited new novel by the author of the beloved *Patience and Sarah.* ISBN 0-930044-81-9 8.95

THE HOUSE AT PELHAM FALLS by Brenda Weathers. 240 pp. Suspenseful Lesbian ghost story.   ISBN 0-930044-79-7   7.95

HOME IN YOUR HANDS by Lee Lynch. 240 pp. More stories from the author of *Old Dyke Tales.*   ISBN 0-930044-80-0   7.95

EACH HAND A MAP by Anita Skeen. 112 pp. Real-life poems that touch us all.   ISBN 0-930044-82-7   6.95

SURPLUS by Sylvia Stevenson. 342 pp. A classic early Lesbian novel.   ISBN 0-930044-78-9   7.95

PEMBROKE PARK by Michelle Martin. 256 pp. Derring-do and daring romance in Regency England. ISBN 0-930044-77-0   7.95

THE LONG TRAIL by Penny Hayes. 248 pp. Vivid adventures of two women in love in the old west.   ISBN 0-930044-76-2   8.95

HORIZON OF THE HEART by Shelley Smith. 192 pp. Hot romance in summertime New England.   ISBN 0-930044-75-4   7.95

AN EMERGENCE OF GREEN by Katherine V. Forrest. 288 pp. Powerful novel of sexual discovery.   ISBN 0-930044-69-X   8.95

THE LESBIAN PERIODICALS INDEX edited by Claire Potter. 432 pp. Author & subject index.   ISBN 0-930044-74-6   29.95

DESERT OF THE HEART by Jane Rule. 224 pp. A classic; basis for the movie *Desert Hearts.*   ISBN 0-930044-73-8   7.95

SPRING FORWARD/FALL BACK by Sheila Ortiz Taylor. 288 pp. Literary novel of timeless love.   ISBN 0-930044-70-3   7.95

FOR KEEPS by Elisabeth Nonas. 144 pp. Contemporary novel about losing and finding love.   ISBN 0-930044-71-1   7.95

TORCHLIGHT TO VALHALLA by Gale Wilhelm. 128 pp. Classic novel by a great Lesbian writer.   ISBN 0-930044-68-1   7.95

LESBIAN NUNS: BREAKING SILENCE edited by Rosemary Curb and Nancy Manahan. 432 pp. Unprecedented autobiographies of religious life.   ISBN 0-930044-62-2   9.95

THE SWASHBUCKLER by Lee Lynch. 288 pp. Colorful novel set in Greenwich Village in the sixties.   ISBN 0-930044-66-5   7.95

MISFORTUNE'S FRIEND by Sarah Aldridge. 320 pp. Historical Lesbian novel set on two continents.   ISBN 0-930044-67-3   7.95

A STUDIO OF ONE'S OWN by Ann Stokes. Edited by Dolores Klaich. 128 pp. Autobiography.   ISBN 0-930044-64-9   7.95

SEX VARIANT WOMEN IN LITERATURE by Jeannette Howard Foster. 448 pp. Literary history. ISBN 0-930044-65-7   8.95

A HOT-EYED MODERATE by Jane Rule. 252 pp. Hard-hitting essays on gay life; writing; art.   ISBN 0-930044-57-6   7.95

INLAND PASSAGE AND OTHER STORIES by Jane Rule. 288 pp. Wide-ranging new collection.   ISBN 0-930044-56-8   7.95

WE TOO ARE DRIFTING by Gale Wilhelm. 128 pp. Timeless Lesbian novel, a masterpiece.   ISBN 0-930044-61-4   6.95

AMATEUR CITY by Katherine V. Forrest. 224 pp. A Kate Delafield mystery. First in a series.   ISBN 0-930044-55-X   7.95

THE SOPHIE HOROWITZ STORY by Sarah Schulman. 176 pp. Engaging novel of madcap intrigue.   ISBN 0-930044-54-1   7.95

THE BURNTON WIDOWS by Vicki P. McConnell. 272 pp. A Nyla Wade mystery, second in the series.   ISBN 0-930044-52-5   7.95

OLD DYKE TALES by Lee Lynch. 224 pp. Extraordinary stories of our diverse Lesbian lives.   ISBN 0-930044-51-7   7.95

DAUGHTERS OF A CORAL DAWN by Katherine V. Forrest. 240 pp. Novel set in a Lesbian new world. ISBN 0-930044-50-9   7.95

THE PRICE OF SALT by Claire Morgan. 288 pp. A milestone novel, a beloved classic.   ISBN 0-930044-49-5   8.95

AGAINST THE SEASON by Jane Rule. 224 pp. Luminous, complex novel of interrelationships.   ISBN 0-930044-48-7   7.95

LOVERS IN THE PRESENT AFTERNOON by Kathleen Fleming. 288 pp. A novel about recovery and growth.
ISBN 0-930044-46-0   8.95

TOOTHPICK HOUSE by Lee Lynch. 264 pp. Love between two Lesbians of different classes.   ISBN 0-930044-45-2   7.95

MADAME AURORA by Sarah Aldridge. 256 pp. Historical novel featuring a charismatic "seer."   ISBN 0-930044-44-4   7.95

CURIOUS WINE by Katherine V. Forrest. 176 pp. Passionate Lesbian love story, a best-seller.   ISBN 0-930044-43-6   7.95

BLACK LESBIAN IN WHITE AMERICA by Anita Cornwell. 141 pp. Stories, essays, autobiography.   ISBN 0-930044-41-X   7.50

CONTRACT WITH THE WORLD by Jane Rule. 340 pp. Powerful, panoramic novel of gay life.   ISBN 0-930044-28-2   7.95

YANTRAS OF WOMANLOVE by Tee A. Corinne. 64 pp. Photos by noted Lesbian photographer.   ISBN 0-930044-30-4   6.95

MRS. PORTER'S LETTER by Vicki P. McConnell. 224 pp. The first Nyla Wade mystery.   ISBN 0-930044-29-0   7.95

TO THE CLEVELAND STATION by Carol Anne Douglas. 192 pp. Interracial Lesbian love story.   ISBN 0-930044-27-4   6.95

THE NESTING PLACE by Sarah Aldridge. 224 pp. A three-woman triangle—love conquers all! ISBN 0-930044-26-6   7.95

THIS IS NOT FOR YOU by Jane Rule. 284 pp. A letter to a beloved is also an intricate novel.   ISBN 0-930044-25-8   7.95

FAULTLINE by Sheila Ortiz Taylor. 140 pp. Warm, funny, literate story of a startling family.   ISBN 0-930044-24-X   6.95

THE LESBIAN IN LITERATURE by Barbara Grier. 3d ed. Foreword by Maida Tilchen. 240 pp. Comprehensive bibliography. Literary ratings; rare photos.   ISBN 0-930044-23-1   7.95

ANNA'S COUNTRY by Elizabeth Lang. 208 pp. A woman finds her Lesbian identity.   ISBN 0-930044-19-3   6.95

PRISM by Valerie Taylor. 158 pp. A love affair between two women in their sixties.   ISBN 0-930044-18-5   6.95

BLACK LESBIANS: AN ANNOTATED BIBLIOGRAPHY
compiled by J.R. Roberts. Foreword by Barbara Smith. 112
pp. Award winning bibliography.   ISBN 0-930044-21-5   5.95

THE MARQUISE AND THE NOVICE by Victoria Ramstetter.
108 pp. A Lesbian Gothic novel.   ISBN 0-930044-16-9   4.95

OUTLANDER by Jane Rule. 207 pp. Short stories and essays
by one of our finest writers.   ISBN 0-930044-17-7   6.95

SAPPHISTRY: THE BOOK OF LESBIAN SEXUALITY by
Pat Califia. 2d edition, revised. 195 pp.   ISBN 0-930044-47-9   7.95

ALL TRUE LOVERS by Sarah Aldridge. 292 pp. Romantic
novel set in the 1930s and 1940s.   ISBN 0-930044-10-X   7.95

A WOMAN APPEARED TO ME by Renee Vivien. 65 pp. A
classic; translated by Jeannette H. Foster. ISBN 0-930044-06-1   5.00

CYTHEREA'S BREATH by Sarah Aldridge. 240 pp. Romantic
novel about women's entrance into medicine.   0-930044-02-9   6.95

TOTTIE by Sarah Aldridge. 181 pp. Lesbian romance in the
turmoil of the sixties.   ISBN 0-930044-01-0   6.95

THE LATECOMER by Sarah Aldridge. 107 pp. A delicate love
story.   ISBN 0-930044-00-2   5.00

ODD GIRL OUT by Ann Bannon   ISBN 0-930044-83-5   5.95
I AM A WOMAN by Ann Bannon.   ISBN 0-930044-84-3   5.95
WOMEN IN THE SHADOWS by Ann Bannon.
                                    ISBN 0-930044-85-1   5.95
JOURNEY TO A WOMAN by Ann Bannon.
                                    ISBN 0-930044-86-X   5.95
BEEBO BRINKER by Ann Bannon   ISBN 0-930044-87-8   5.95

Legendary novels written in the fifties and sixties,
set in the gay mecca of Greenwich Village.

VOLUTE BOOKS

JOURNEY TO FULFILLMENT   Early classics by Valerie   3.95
A WORLD WITHOUT MEN   Taylor: The Erika Frohmann   3.95
RETURN TO LESBOS   series.   3.95

These are just a few of the many Naiad Press titles—we are the oldest
and largest lesbian/feminist publishing company in the world. Please
request a complete catalog. We offer personal service; we encourage and
welcome direct mail orders from individuals who have limited access to
bookstores carrying our publications.

$$3 \times 3 = 9$$
$$2 \quad 4$$
$$1 \times 4 \quad \overline{13}$$
$$\quad\quad 10$$
$$1 \times 10 \quad \overline{23}$$
$$1 \times 7 \quad \overline{7}$$
$$\quad\quad 30$$